AF443019

White Stiletto Press

Dedication

This book is dedicated to our Keith,
who fought a heroic battle against cancer,
which he sadly lost on the 7 September 2013.

Keith was more Boon than Bonanza but
without a doubt the bravest cowboy I know.

Sleep well, mate, you've earned it.
Jaynee and James are in good hands.
You'll be forever in our hearts.

Contents

Chapter one

Vance surveyed the ranch from on top of the hill overlooking the valley, his right leg crossed over the pommel, the horn digging into his thigh. Leaning forward, he stroked along the length of his horse's sweat-dampened neck, mumbling soothing nonsense as he stared down at his home. He'd ridden Goliath hard across the south pasture in an attempt to clear his head, and he knew the animal would be grateful for the breather. A chuckle rumbled in his chest as Goliath dipped his head to nibble at the grass, obviously taking full advantage of Vance's pensive mood. Could the horse sense he wasn't exactly eager to return home? Vance wouldn't be surprised.

Gazing down at the ranch, the familiar flash of pride washed through him. Wolf Creek was a little Texan town sixty miles from the hustle and bustle of Austin, where life moved along at a sedate pace, a far cry from the big city. Benjamin Wolf, Vance's great-great grandfather, had been one of the town's original founders in 1878 and there had always been a Wolf in residence at Wolf Creek Ranch. As far as Vance was concerned, that's how it was going to stay.

Some of the cattle had been spooked during last night's storm and broken through one of the fences, and Vance had spent most of the morning herding them off his neighbor's ranch. Thankfully he'd known the Carters, who'd owned the land along the south side of Wolf Creek since he was a kid, so he'd had help from Jake Carter's men to round up the wanderers. Not that the same could be said for the ranch that stretched away on the other side of the shallow creek bed that gave Vance's ranch its name. Sweet Meadow Ranch had been owned by the Gartons for forty years until a year ago when old man Garton had died. His son, Malcolm, had moved off the farm as soon as he could, and his father had barely been in the ground before he'd sold the spread to some businessman no one had ever heard of out of New York. Two weeks later Andrew Blackwell had moved in, bringing more money than Wolf Creek had ever seen, charming his way into the good graces of the townsfolk, and lining the pockets of the local council and sheriff's offices.

Hell, he'd even charmed Vance's parents, Jacob and Audrey Wolf, for a while, too—but not him. Vance remembered the night Blackwell had sat at their dinner table, eating his momma's roast off his grandmother's china with the best silver. He'd seemed nice enough; said all the right things, made all the right jokes, but Vance had noted, with a sense of unease, that Blackwell's smile never reached his eyes. Cold, dead eyes—like a shark's.

It had been during dessert, his momma's apple cobbler if he remembered it right, that Blackwell had expressed an interest in Wolf Creek. Vance's father had laughed it off and they'd continued with the meal, but Vance hadn't missed the flicker of annoyance Blackwell hadn't quite been able to disguise before the subject had been changed. Throughout the rest of the evening Vance's first impression of the man hadn't improved and, two weeks later, when they received the first formal offer from Blackwell's solicitors, he'd known he'd been right to go with his gut instinct.

Once every formal offer made through his solicitors had been refused, Blackwell turned to slightly less orthodox methods in an attempt to persuade Vance's father to sell. Methods that started with holes made in the fences, followed by a few head of cattle disappearing overnight, to the herd's water bins being poisoned and then the final straw for Vance, the barn housing their horses being set on fire in the dead of night. If it hadn't been for the fact that a couple of the hands had decided to stay over that night in the old bunkhouse and had awoken them, the barn would have burned down to the ground. They'd managed to get most of the horses out and douse the flames, but if the wind had been blowing in any other direction, the fire could have reached the house.

At first Vance had climbed bareback onto Goliath and turned him toward Blackwell's place, having every intention of beating the son of a bitch within an inch of his life. If his mother hadn't stood in front of him with his father's shotgun, he would have—but not even he was brave enough to stand up to Audrey Wolf with a loaded firearm in her hands. That and her insistence that no Wolf had ever gone to jail and she'd be damned if her son would be the first.

The sheriff had been informed, of course, but he was an asshole who couldn't quite cut it as a city beat cop with an instruction manual and a flashlight; so the money he received from Blackwell to turn a blind eye was the best offer he'd ever had—and he did his job well. Once the law had become involved, so to speak, Vance had thought that Blackwell would step back, but he hadn't. His harassment had continued, and it was three months into his campaign that Jacob Wolf had suffered his first heart attack.

Brought on by stress, the doctors said. *No shit!* had been Vance's response. Again, it had taken every ounce of will his mother possessed to keep him from doing something stupid the first time he saw his father lying against those hospital sheets, so pale, so still—so old. He'd never thought of his father as aging like everyone else. His father was formidable, a superhero who rode over the plains on his trusty steed, roping steers and herding cattle, a pack of chewing tobacco in his top pocket at all times. Not this shell of a man with electrodes everywhere and veins a stark blue through almost transparent skin. They'd thought he'd been getting stronger and the doctors had talked about him coming home. But the night before he was scheduled to be discharged, Jacob had suffered another heart attack in the early hours of the morning, and they hadn't been able to save him.

Goliath shifted beneath him as his fist clenched around the reins. Vance clicked his tongue and patted the majestic beast's neck by way of apology. In the six months since he'd buried his father, the cattle had continued to disappear from Wolf land, and Vance continued to report his losses to the sheriff's office. Not that it did any good. All he could do was send his crew out to fix the fences and round up any cattle that bore the Wolf Creek brand.

If Blackwell thought Vance would be run off his own property or would just hand him the deeds and slink away with his tail between his legs, he was in for a surprise. Vance Wolf had no intention of allowing *any* Blackwell to ever set foot on his land again.

Vance could fix as many fences as Blackwell cared to sabotage, but he couldn't replace the herd as quickly as it was being thinned, and the ranch had to make money—fast. He scratched at the back of his neck where the sun was making a valiant attempt to burn a hole through his skin. When the idea of opening the ranch to businesses as a team-building experience had been pitched to him by his mother, he'd reacted as she must have known he would—with a disbelieving stare followed by a colorful refusal. Of course, she had gone on to make several good points. Number one, they were losing cattle they didn't have the money to replace. Number two, those idiots in the city would pay a buck load for a genuine cowboy experience. And number three, *she* had the controlling interest in the ranch, not him.

Vance's cell vibrated in his back pocket and he sighed heavily. The first of many he was sure he would be heaving over the next few days. He fished the sliver of metal from the confines of his jeans and cursed softly as his mother's face flashed on the screen. Not that he was cursing her per se, he wasn't an idiot for God's sake. He pressed the button to accept the call and put the phone to his ear. "Mornin', Mom."

"Don't you 'mornin' Mom' me," Audrey Wolf said frostily. "Where the hell are you? Gabby is gonna be back from the airport with the guests any minute and if you're not here to greet them, we'll be getting off on the wrong foot."

"I'm just checking the rest of the fencing along the

creek side." Vance winced at the sound of his mother's scoff at his bald lie. She was his mother for God's sake, she'd heard him lie before. "I'll be in soon. I'm sure you'll be able to meet and greet a few businessmen just fine by yourself."

"Vance Benjamin Elvis Wolf." Audrey used his full name, even the embarrassing one, so he knew he was pretty much in deep shit. "Unless you want it handed to you on a platter, I suggest you get that stubborn ass of yours back to the house as if it's on fire. Do I make myself clear?"

Recognizing the no nonsense tone of his mother's voice that usually came just before a threatened trip to the woodshed during his youth, Vance emitted yet another sigh and replied through gritted teeth, "Yes, Momma." What else was he going to say? No? To Audrey Wolf? They both knew that, even at thirty-two years old, the chances of him being brave enough to defy her were a million to one.

After he'd pressed the button to end the call, Vance cursed loudly into the air, letting the wind carry his displeasure across the valley. Ten minutes was all he needed... just ten minutes alone with Andrew Blackwell to stop this foolishness. *Who're you kidding? Ten minutes alone with Blackwell would end with twenty-five years to life for you up at Huntsville.* His inner voice had a point.

Vance gathered the reins in his leather-gloved hands and Goliath reluctantly ceased his contemplative chewing of the sweet blades of grass at his feet. A gentle tap of Vance's heels against ebony flanks were all the instructions Goliath needed, and the horse trotted down the hill in the direction of the house.

Goliath reached the barn just in time for Vance to see Gabby's gun-metal gray Silverado pull up in front of the long single story homestead. His grandfather had built in the Forties, after tearing down the original house built by Benjamin Wolf all those years ago. Vance slid off Goliath's back, gritting his teeth so hard his jaw ached. The sight of five suited men clambering out of the truck and up the porch steps sent acid into his gullet, and he swallowed it down with a grimace. He would sure as shit bet that when Benjamin Wolf laid the foundations to the original homestead, he hadn't ever imagined city folk crossing its threshold. Worse still… city folk *pretending* to be cowboys.

"Be nice."

Vance passed the reins to Walt, his father's right hand man who was practically part of the furniture at Wolf Creek he'd been there for so long and put on his best butter wouldn't melt look. "I'm always nice. Just a sweet ole pussycat, you know that."

"If by sweet ole pussycat you mean rabid tiger, then yeah, that's you to a T," Walt said with a sarcastic drawl, then turned and led Goliath toward the barn, muttering under his breath as he walked.

Vance stretched his arms high over his head and then squared his shoulders. Taking a deep breath, he strode purposefully toward the house where his mother's sternest glare and morons with more money than sense waited for him. A slow predatory grin spread across his face as he stomped up the porch steps. If they wanted to be cowboys, he was more than happy to give them the *full* experience.

Inside the house he headed down the long corridor to his mother's domain, the huge kitchen diner where she fed the ranch hands twice a day. Although now the suits had arrived, she would be adding dinner to the menu. He paused just before the open doorway and leaned against the wall as he listened to his mother introduce their—he searched for a word that wasn't derogatory and reluctantly settled for—guests to Wolf Creek.

"You'll have to forgive my son, gentleman. We had some cows go a-wandering during the storm last night, but he should be here any minute," Audrey Wolf said, the welcoming smile audible in her voice, followed by the chink of glass. Vance rolled his eyes. He knew she'd been planning on making some of her Country Fayre winning lemonade. Didn't all those city types have bottles of Perrier on demand? He'd bet not a single one of them would appreciate the effort she'd gone to.

"You must all be parched from your trip," Audrey said brightly. "I'm afraid the heat can be a little more cloying out here than in the city and last night's storm did nothing to clear the air, so I made y'all something cool. Please, help yourselves. It's the best in the state, if I do say so myself."

"Wow, that's wonderful, Mrs Wolf." Vance's ears pricked up at the sound of the male voice after a few moments silence in which the men were obviously sampling his mother's lemonade. It was a deep, rich Yankee drawl with a soft lilting undertone that lifted the fine hairs on the nape of his neck. "As the senior executive, I'd like to extend our appreciation to you for your hospitality before the week starts—just in case we're all too exhausted to be able to extend anything by the end of it."

"Why thank you, Adam." Vance could practically hear his mother preening. "I'm sure Vance has plenty in store for you. Isn't that right, honey?" His mother raised her voice on the last. Dammit, she'd known he was there the whole time? How? He took off his Stetson and pushed himself away from the wall, then strolled into the kitchen as nonchalantly as he could to meet his mother's gaze. She smiled sweetly at him, but he wasn't fooled. He could tell by the mere lift of her chin that he was going to have a new one ripped when they were alone. "You never could remember that creaky floorboard right before the doorway."

Vance crossed the room and leaned down to give his diminutive mother a kiss on her smooth cheek. "Nope," he said, with a rueful shake of his head and an apologetic smile. "That floorboard's got me in more trouble than I care to remember."

"Gentleman, this is my son, Vance Wolf, and he'll be taking good care of you this weekend. Ain't that right?" His mother's tone held a note of warning that only he would recognize, and Vance nodded, taking his first proper look at the men watching them with obvious interest.

"Absolutely," Vance replied, his gaze measuring up each man in turn. "I'm gonna make sure each and every one of you is completely—" He paused as his gaze settled on the man leaning against the counter and found himself staring into a pair of cool gray eyes, or were they a dirty blue? *Since when do you give a shit about eye-color? You usually only care to see the back of their heads while you're fucking 'em into the mattress.* His inner voice may be right, but that didn't mean he couldn't appreciate the finer things in life, and this guy was fine with a capital-fucking-F. Short light-brown hair, neatly styled back from his forehead. Wide eyes he'd already established as a pale gray slash dirty blue, above an aquiline nose and full, luscious lips that looked so soft, Vance had to swallow down the sudden urge to find out if it were in fact true. Finished off with the merest hint of a stubbled beard that Vance would have laid money on feeling like heaven against his skin. He deliberately moistened his lips with the tip of his tongue and was pleased to note the immediate darkening of those pretty eyes in response, and continued, the single word heavy on his tongue with hidden meaning, "*Satisfied.*"

Vance grinned in amusement when the hottie blushed and shifted his weight from one foot to another and dropped his gaze to stare into the glass of lemonade he held. *Maybe this week ain't gonna be so bad after all.*

Chapter two

Adam dumped his bag on the bed—if you could call it that. It was more like an ancient roll-away and the mattress was barely six inches thick in a twelve by eight room with a washstand in one corner and a dresser in the other. The bunkhouse had been built close to the side of the long one story house, leaving about six feet between the buildings, which was probably no more distance than you wanted to traverse during the winter months. Yet far enough to ensure both the family and the crew had their own space. Not exactly the Hilton, but then he hadn't been expecting a five star resort. He sat down on the bed and winced at the creaking of the springs. The other thing he hadn't been expecting was Vance Wolf. The way the man had been described, he'd envisioned some kind of grizzled Lee Marvin type with a shaggy beard and a bag of chewing tobacco. Nothing could have prepared him for the handsome man with the chiseled jaw and moss-green gaze that had lazily drifted over him from head to toe, touching everywhere in between.

Vance had obviously liked what he saw, because he'd made no attempt to disguise his appreciation, and his voice—dear God, his *voice*. Adam gave a full body shudder at the memory of the deep timbre that sounded as though it should have come from a throat that had been abused by cigar smoke and hard liquor for thirty years; edged with a husky crackle that had the fine hair on the back of Adam's neck standing to attention.

Adam had felt the warmth flood his cheeks under the intensity of the cowboy's gaze, and downed his lemonade in three swallows, unable to ignore the wicked gleam in those green depths, or the tickling fingers of answering attraction dancing up and down his spine. He had the feeling that, if he wasn't careful, he might just be in danger of Vance Wolf roping *him* this week instead of the cows. But that was *not* what he was here for. Goddamnit, he didn't *want* to be here at all, and he'd bet on Vance Wolf wanting to hang him with that rope instead of pulling him in if he knew the truth.

Lifting his gaze, Adam caught sight of his reflection in the mirror above the washstand. He'd worried there would be a slim chance Vance or his mother might recognize him, but he'd been assured the Wolfs were not exactly the type to read the society pages or the gossip columns. Adam sighed heavily and picked up his cell, stabbing out the numbers and then waiting for the call to connect. He didn't even give the woman who answered a chance to get out the full name of the company before he snapped instructions at her.

"Andrew Blackwell."

"May I ask who's calling?"

"His son."

The wait for his father to come on the line was minimal. Knowing him like he did, Adam knew the man had more than likely been sitting by the phone willing it to ring. Probably calling him all the names he could think of and making a few up, too. But then that wasn't out of the ordinary where Adam was concerned. Well, could kiss his ass. They'd spent a good deal of the afternoon around the dining-table listening to Vance and Audrey go over the history of the ranch, and the activities they had planned for their stay.

In an attempt to avoid Vance's stare as much as possible, Adam had gazed around the large typical farmhouse kitchen. The room was obviously Audrey's domain, her stamp was all over it and at any other time he would have probably appreciated the decor and history lesson more—but not today. Today he'd been hot—hot and pissed, an unpleasant combination.

Graham, the second in command of his department, had given him a thumbs up from across the kitchen, and Adam had resisted giving him the finger in return. He'd been sorely tempted but doubted the gesture would create the best first impression for Audrey, who had so warmly welcomed them into her home. Of course, she too would have kicked his ass all the way back down the three mile drive to the entrance of Wolf Creek, if she'd known she sat across the table from Andrew Blackwell's youngest son. Not that she should. Hell, the members of his own team didn't even know who he was.

After university, his father had forced him into the business. Adam had wanted to be a veterinarian, specializing in horses and cattle, but the great Andrew Blackwell wouldn't hear of it. He was a Blackwell, and he would work for the family business, like his brother, his father and his grandfather before him. No son of his was going to spend the day elbow-deep in a cow's ass, no sirree. The fight that followed had been their worst ever. Ending with Adam on his knees from the blow to his jaw from his father's clenched fist, and his head pounding where it had been hit by the eagle paperweight his father had thrown at him. He'd walked from the room with his blood on his hands and his fate sealed. That Monday he'd started work in the mailroom under his mother's maiden name. His father hadn't liked it, but Adam had stood his ground and refused to set foot in the building if the staff knew he was a Blackwell. Surprisingly, his father had agreed and had pretty much left him alone, which is how Adam liked it, both at the office and at home. Now, three years later, he was the head of the marketing department and had earned every promotion without any help from the big boss man.

Which is why he'd known he was right to be suspicious when his father had called him into his office two weeks ago. When his father had said he was sending Adam and his team on a team building exercise to Wolf Creek Ranch to be cowboys for a week, he desperately tried to come up with a plausible excuse as to why he was unavailable. Like… having his colon flushed… waxing his testicles… or a pre-booked castration he simply couldn't miss. Anything that would be less painful than spending time 'on the range'.

So here he was. In a house full of the same self-important assholes he couldn't wait to get away from on a Friday, with a week of hog-tying and cow-tipping stretched ahead of him like a black hole. Adam ran his hand through his hair in agitation. He could already feel his very soul being sucked into the abyss of learning the words to Oklahoma and shouting yippee-kai-ay at random moments. Although he was definitely more the Bruce Willis in a dirty vest and bare feet type of yippee-kai-ay-er than the Calamity Jane one—or in his case, Calamity John—even if Howard Keel had looked damned fine in those chaps.

Not that the week itself was the suspicious part of the scenario. It was what his father had instructed him to do next that filled him with a sense of unease. While he was there, he was to keep a close eye on Vance Wolf, get the lay of the land and find out exactly how deep a pile of shit the ranch was in. When he'd asked his father why, the answer had been short and not so sweet—it was none of his fucking business. He was to just do as he was told—and under no circumstances was anyone to know who he was, or where he was from.

"At last! Where the hell have you been?"

"And hello to you, too, Dad." Adam didn't even attempt to keep the sarcasm from his voice.

"No one likes a smartass, Adam," Andrew Blackwell replied, his annoyance loud and clear. "I told you to call me as soon as you arrived."

"I know," Adam said coldly. "You also told me no one was supposed to know who I am. This is the first time I've been alone since I got to JFK this morning."

"Watch your tone, boy." There was a slight pause before his father spoke again. "Have you met Wolf and his mother?"

"Yes, I have. They seem like nice people," Adam prevaricated.

"Don't be fooled. Vance Wolf is a cold son of a bitch."

"I guess it takes one to know one." The silence that followed his caustic remark was heavy, foreboding, and for the first time since his father had answered his call,

Adam felt the familiar fingers of fear curling deep in his gut. He moistened his suddenly dry lips and mumbled into the phone. "I'm sorry." God, how he hated the way his father could turn him into a scared kid desperate for approval, terrified of incurring his wrath and the back of his hand—all without saying a word. He swallowed hard, knowing his father was stretching out the silence to amp up his distress, and he was on the verge of losing his fucking mind when his father finally spoke.

"Listen good, boy. You're there to do a job. You're not there to form your own opinion of those people, do you understand me? I want to know every last detail about that ranch. From the state of their accounts to how much horseshit they shovel. I want that land, Adam, and you're going to help me get it—by *any* means necessary."

"What are you talking about?" Adam's stomach sank into his shoes.

"You know what I'm talking about." His father's voice was a sneer. "Did you honestly think I wouldn't find out *what* you are? Not that it was any great surprise… just another thing to add to the long list of disappointments. You're just like your mother—weak. Do whatever you have to do to get what I need, and I do mean *whatever*. I'm assuming that won't be a problem. I hear you people don't much care where you stick your dick."

The silence of a dead line echoed like thunder in his ear, so many thoughts pin-balling around his skull he couldn't hang onto a single one of them. He'd been so careful. How could he know? *How do you think?* The voice of his subconscious echoed in his ears. *How does he find out anything?* Of course. Adam rubbed a hand over his face. He'd had him followed. The kind of men his father hired would have no problem digging around in his private life and reporting back to the big boss man with relish.

Adam flopped back onto the bed and stared up at a cobweb stretching from the ceiling to the shade covering the light bulb. After all this time he supposed nothing his father did should surprise him, and yet the instruction that he should *prostitute* himself. Wow, that was a new one, even for a sadistic son of a bitch like Andrew Blackwell. Adam frowned. What was it about this place? What the hell was so special about Wolf Creek? It wasn't exactly South Fork, for God's sake. More like South Fork's cousin, the black sheep of the family, who didn't get a Christmas card.

What did his father, the owner of the biggest acquisitions and mergers company in New York, want with a two-bit cattle ranch? Adam sat up and swung his legs over the side of the bed, his boots hitting the floor with a satisfying thwack. He had no idea what his father was up to—but he was going to find out.

Chapter three

"Now, now, settle down, boys."

Vance grinned at his mother as he carried the massive saucepan from the stove to the head of the table. She was in her element at mealtimes, flitting around the kitchen like a restless butterfly, alighting for a few moments here and there and then fluttering off again. Around the table sat Walt, who had his own set of rooms in the rambling bunkhouse, Cory and Jarvis, the other two resident ranch hands and their five paying guests from the Big Apple itself.

Taking his seat next to his mother, Vance gazed at the assembled diners and he tried not to laugh at the businessmen in their pristine polo shirts and casual pants, beside Walt, Cory and Travis in their jeans, chaps and plaid button downs. Although Audrey drew the line at spurs at the table, you could definitely tell who the cowboys were and who were the civilians. He really needed to get these guys out on the range and dust 'em up a little—his gaze fell on Adam Prentiss—some more than others.

"If you pass the plates to me one by one, I'll serve," Audrey said, standing at the head of the table and holding out her hand for Vance's plate. "What we have on offer tonight, gentlemen, is the specialty of the house. Wolf stew is a recipe that has been handed down from my late husband's great-grandmother." She tipped them a wink as she ladled chunks of meat and vegetables onto Vance's plate. "And yes, it did originally contain actual wolf. But this one's made from our own beef, so I hope you're hungry."

"Hell, yeah, Mz Audrey."

Vance shot a glance at Cory who sat clenching his plate with eager hands. "You're always hungry," he said, putting his dinner in front of him and then taking the plate from the man beside him—who he thought was named Graham. A less cowboy-esque man you were ever likely to meet. A man in his fifties who looked like he would rather be anywhere else but here. He also gave off an air of nervous timidity that had Vance wondering how the guy even coped in an office, never mind out on the range. What the hell had his mother gotten him into?

After all the plates had been filled, Audrey put three plates of biscuits on the table then took her own seat. She held her hand out to Vance and he slipped his fingers in hers before half-turning and offering his other hand to Graham. Who looked at his open palm with a bemused expression on his face. Vance raised a sardonic eyebrow and glanced around the table at the less than comfortable men staring back at him, except for Walt, Cory and Travis, who were already holding hands. "I dunno how you big city types do it, but out here we say Grace. And since your boss is paying through the nose for the Wolf Creek experience, you'd better get your cowboy on."

Adam Prentiss put his hand in Travis's and nodded to the other members of his team. "You heard the man. Saddle up."

Vance lifted his chin slightly in acknowledgement then closed his eyes and bowed his head as his mother said Grace, her tone soft, yet firm, giving thanks for the food on their table. A thousand memories skittered in fast forward behind his closed lids. When he was a boy this was always his favorite time of the day. Listening to the rise and fall of his mother's lilting tone as she thanked the Almighty that they'd made it safely through another day, with enough food on the table to satisfy hungry bellies, and enough love to keep the corners of the coldest heart warm. And the smiles and laughter from the men around the table had always created a longing within him for the day he would be able to join them at work on the land he loved so much. At the mumbled amen, Vance released the hands he held and immediately made a bee-line for the biscuits closest to him.

"Vance, remember your manners."

"Sorry, Momma." Vance mumbled around the huge bite he'd taken. He reached out for another and his fingers collided with those of Adam Prentiss, who'd obviously realized that if you didn't eat fast, you didn't eat at all. His lips twitched at the equal speed with which Adam dropped the biscuit they'd both headed for, as though it were white hot. He picked up the biscuit and held it out to him. The man was definitely affected by him. You'd have to be deaf, blind and stupid not to know that, but he was obviously going all out to disguise his attraction. Why would he—?

A light bulb switched on above Vance's head. His colleagues didn't know he was gay. Seriously? He himself had walked into the kitchen on his fourteenth birthday, sat down to breakfast and calmly announced it to his remarkably unsurprised mother and unimpressed father, whose only responses had been, "Jacob, you owe me fifty bucks" and "Does this mean I have to change the Longhorn tickets to the Ice Capades?" respectively. Being gay wasn't exactly a big deal nowadays, so why was he hiding it?

Adam took the biscuit from him and Vance smirked at the way he carefully avoided touching Vance's hand as he did so. Yeah—he was affected by him alright. "I'm sorry?" Vance turned to Graham on his left, suddenly aware the man was speaking to him.

"I was just wondering what we could expect?"

Vance felt sorry for the guy. He looked as though he would rather be absolutely anywhere else but at this table. "Well, gentlemen, we're a cattle ranch, so most of our day is spent on horseback. I'm assuming ya'll can ride?" His gaze flitted around the group and he inwardly groaned at the blank faces staring back at him. "Seriously? *None* of you?"

"I can ride," Adam mumbled around a mouthful of stew.

"I ain't talking about BMW's."

"Neither am I."

Vance had to hand it to Adam, he could obviously give as good as he got. It was just a shame he didn't know he was dealing with a master.

"I had a few riding lessons when I was a kid," one of the other men said with a shrug. "But I lost interest when I got my first set of golf clubs."

"Momma," Vance sighed heavily. "You'd better make up some of Gamma's special rub. I think we're gonna need it tomorrow night."

"Special rub?" Graham asked, his fork pausing

halfway between his plate and his mouth.

"Yep," Vance nodded. "For the blisters."

"Blisters?" Golf Club Guy asked. "I thought we were going to ride, why would we get blisters?"

"Oh, it ain't for your feet, honey," Audrey piped up, dropping a wink at the now white-faced man.

Vance burst out laughing and Cory choked on his stew, until one by one everyone around the table had joined in and the air in the kitchen felt immediately lighter. He dipped his biscuit in the meat and vegetable rich stew in front of him and popped it into his mouth, his gaze briefly meeting Adam's. Vance's gut tightened as a bolt of heat surged through him. Embarrassed and nervous, Adam Prentiss was gorgeous. With his face lit by laughter and a grin that would have melted the hardest heart, he was breathtaking. A sudden image of Adam spread out on his mattress, honey-colored skin stark against the white of his sheets, all trace of laughter gone, leaving only raw, primal need.

Mentally shaking his head free of the image, mainly because he really didn't want a boner at the dinner table, Vance concentrated on his food. What the fuck was wrong with him and this waxing lyrical honey-colored shit? He didn't have time for that kind of crap. His plate was already on maximum overload, the last thing he needed was some suit messing with his head.

"This beef is fantastic, Mrs Wolf," from white-faced guy, whose name, it turned out, was Phil. "It melts in your mouth." His smile was appreciative. "But I bet that's got more to do with your cooking than the meat itself."

"A little of both, Philip," Audrey said with a nod. "A little of both. You know, my momma always said if you add a little love into each dish it makes it taste better. I like to throw in a quick prayer at the last minute, too and it seems to have worked out alright for me so far. But then my late husband always said there was something in the soil here at Wolf Creek that produced the best grass in all of Texas, so I reckon it's a combination of all three."

Walt sat back in his chair and clapped his hands over his rotund stomach. "Mz Audrey, you have outdone yourself once again. I don't think I'm gonna be able to move for a week!"

"Pretty much an average day on the farm for you then, Walt. 'Siderin' I ain't seen you move since *last* week," Cory said, the tease evident in his voice.

"Don't make me put you over my knee, son," Walt warned, his bristled beard bristling even more than usual.

"I don't think there's much danger of that." Travis joined in, grinning mischievously at Cory. "There ain't room for you *and* his belly."

Everyone laughed at the wordplay between the three men and Vance shook his head fondly at his crew. Walt was like a second father to him. Vance remembered sitting in front of Walt atop old Blue, the horse Walt had when Vance was maybe four or five. He'd sit there and hold onto the reins, feeling like king of the hill as they rode across the ranch, listening to Walt barking out orders to the ranch hands. Watching his father rope cows with a single throw of the lasso, filling Vance with a sense of worshipful awe.

Mopping up the last vestiges of gravy on his plate with what was left of his third biscuit, Vance took the same stance as Walt and patted his stomach, which gurgled contentedly now it was full. "Well, gentlemen, there was a time Momma would have had you all doing the dishes by hand, but nowadays we take it in turns to clear the table and load the dishwasher. I warn you now, leave her kitchen in a mess and you'll be worrying about more than blisters. Now, if you'll excuse me, I've got a mare about to foal that needs tending to. If I were you, I'd try and get a good night's sleep." He grinned as he stood up and crossed to the back door, pausing as he opened it and throwing over his shoulder, "You're gonna need it."

The cool night air lifted his hair off his forehead as Vance strolled past the corral to the barn, their guests forefront in his mind. How in the hell was he supposed to turn them into cowboys? It wasn't even as if he had good solid material to work with. Vance had no idea who their boss was, but he was pretty sure he was laughing his ass off right about now, at his employees' expense. Team building? He'd be lucky if he managed to send them all back in one piece. He chuckled to himself as he walked into the barn. Poor Graham had looked decidedly green when he'd mentioned Gamma's special rub. Unfortunately for him, Vance hadn't been kidding. The chances of any of the men making it through the day without getting saddle-sore was a wager he was not willing to lose money on.

Vance walked through the barn, reaching out to rub the more curious noses appearing over the stall doors. He patted Jupiter softly as he passed, but found his progress halted by the teeth that gently grabbed onto his sleeve. Vance grinned and scratched at Jupiter's ears. He was a big old bay with a penchant for peppermints, hence the nibbling at Vance's top pocket, where he usually kept them. "What're you looking for? As if I didn't know," Vance said, nudging the horse's nose from his shirt. "I'm all out, buddy. You'll have to make do with hay like everybody else." He chuckled as Jupiter made his opinion clear by snorting in his face. "I'll be sure to give the management your message. Now go on, I've got to see to Midnight. You'll get your sugar shock tomorrow." Giving Jupiter one last scratch, Vance walked on until he reached the last stall.

Midnight paced up and down restlessly, her heavy belly hanging low. Vance clicked his tongue against his teeth and her ears pricked up immediately. He opened her stall door and stepped inside, closing it behind him. "Hello, beautiful," he said, keeping his voice low and soothing. He smoothed his hands over her bulging side and laid his cheek against her velvety hide. "Are you being good for your momma in there? We've been waiting a long time to meet you, but you need to sit tight for a few more days, you hear me? Just a few more days." Vance felt the life inside her move, and he closed his eyes on a sigh of relief. This was Midnight's third pregnancy but the first she had carried to term.

"She's gorgeous."

Vance started at the sound of Adam's voice. He'd been so lost in the miracle growing inside of Midnight that he hadn't even heard the man approach. Straightening, he turned on his heel to find Adam leaning on the stall door, a soft smile playing around his lips. "That she is," Vance said on a laugh. "And she knows it. She's a rescue. I got a phone call from the sanctuary in Austin about six years ago. She'd been found tied to a stake with barely enough rope to move her head. No food. No water. No shelter. Not to mention six months pregnant. She was so emaciated she lost the foal. Vet reckoned she hadn't eaten in weeks."

"My God." Adam shook his head in amazement. "How can anyone let an animal suffer like that? I've never been able to understand how people can be so cruel to something so defenseless."

Vance raised an eyebrow at the vehemence of Adam's tone. "Did you grow up around animals?"

"Not really." Adam ran a hand through his dark blond hair and Vance couldn't help but follow the fall of the strands through his fingers. "My grandparents had a farm in Iowa. My mom and I used to go there sometimes."

"So, you're more of a city boy."

"For my sins."

Vance let his gaze wander the length of Adam's body, real slow, noting the blush high on Adam's cheekbones when he reached his face. "I can't believe you've committed too many of those," he drawled, snaking out his tongue to moisten his lips, not missing the way Adam's gaze lingered on his mouth at the movement.

"I've had my share." Adam's tone had cooled a couple of hundred degrees, leaving Vance in no doubt that the flirting part of the conversation was over, even though it had barely begun. "I came out to ask you to take it easy on the guys, especially Graham. He's taking early retirement in six weeks and I don't want him to spend the first few months of it in traction."

"I'm sure your boss didn't send you out here to sit on the porch and drink lemonade for a week," Vance said, patting Midnight's neck for the last time. Crossing the stall, he stopped at the stall door and kept his gaze firmly locked on Adam's until the man straightened and stepped back, allowing Vance to open the door and then latch it behind him.

"No, and we don't expect to," Adam replied, crossing his arms. Vance bit back a snort of laughter. If he thought that was enough to form a barrier between them, he was sorely mistaken. Not that he was going to prove the point right now. "I'm just asking you to show a bit of compassion for some suits who've probably never even seen a horse up close, never mind ridden the damn range on one."

"Well, you seem mighty close to your colleagues there, Mr Prentiss. Your concern for them is touching. Or are you worried it's your own ass that'll be paying the price when *you're* the one who can't keep up." Vance couldn't resist throwing out the bait and Adam snatched at it—and ran with it.

"Oh, I can keep up, *cowboy*. The question is—can *you*?" With that, Adam turned on his heel and strode from the barn, each step heavy with indignation.

Vance chuckled as he watched Adam's retreat, unable not to wonder what that tight little ass would feel like filling his palms. Had the city boy thrown down? Did he honestly think Vance wouldn't take it for the challenge it obviously was? The slow grin curving his lips was predatory and his voice echoed around the barn on the still night air. "Can I keep up? You just watch me."

Chapter four

It was the apocalypse. Adam could come up with no other explanation for the horrendous banging echoing around his skull. He reluctantly opened his eyes, half expecting to see the horrific devastation of the end of the world around him—but no such luck. He was *still* in the sparsely decorated room he'd gone to sleep in the night before, and the apocalypse was in fact the harsh tinny clanging of what must be the biggest bell on the planet.

Adam reached out to the tiny nightstand, felt around for his watch and picked it up. Blinking at the dial as it swam into focus, Adam groaned, shoved his expensive timepiece under the pillow, then pulled the covers up over his head. Five am? *Seriously?* He didn't even know there *was* a five am for God's sake. This exercise was supposed to give the team a boost, not crush them into the dirt—it was goddamned inhuman. He closed his eyes and snuggled under the crisp white sheets and was well on his way back to dreamland when a heavy fist banged on the door to his room. Startled from his half doze he sat bolt upright in bed, his eyes wide. His heartbeat fast and hard against his ribcage.

"I know you're awake, Prentiss." Vance's voice was rough and caused goose bumps to break out on Adam's skin. "Get your ass outta there, or you'll be riding out on an empty stomach. Breakfast is hitting the table in ten minutes, or is that not long enough for you to fix your hair?"

"Fuck off," Adam mumbled beneath his breath before clearing his throat and indicating he was up in a slightly politer fashion. Although he could still hear the *fuck off* in his tone and judging by the rich chuckle from outside his door, so could Vance Wolf. Adam swung his legs over the side of the bed and winced at the coolness of the wood against his bare feet. God, the cowboy was irritating, and sexy, and annoying, and sexy, and full of himself, and sexy—Adam stopped that train of thought in its tracks and scrubbed his fingers through his hair.

Last night in the barn Adam had forced himself to stand his ground against the heat in Vance Wolf's gaze. The insolent way he'd looked at him, with no attempt to hide the thoughts behind those green eyes had Adam's toes curling in his expensive loafers—and it had taken every ounce of willpower not to close the gap between them and show the fucking tease exactly who he was dealing with. If he thought Adam was some sensitive bottom who'd do as he was told—the confident cowboy had better think again. Despite his father's condescending comment on the phone last night, Adam happened to be *very* particular about where he stuck his dick. But he did like to make sure that those who were lucky enough to find out, never forgot it. Not that he had any intention of following his father's instructions regarding his dick. Sure, there'd been a definite instant attraction between him and Vance Wolf, to deny it would be a lie. But that didn't mean he was about to bend over and stick his ass in the air just because the cowboy tipped his hat at him, and certainly not because his father hoped there would be some pillow talk he could use to get his hands on the ranch.

"Time's running out, Prentiss!"

Adam gave the door and the man outside it the finger and then stood up. He stretched his arms high above his head and groaned at the crack of his back and complaint of tense muscles after sleeping on the thin mattress. Still, he supposed it could have been worse. His father could have decided he wanted an Alaskan fishing village, and then they'd not only be tired but freezing their asses off as well.

He grabbed his wash bag, opened the door and headed down the hall to the bathroom, knocking loudly before he pushed at the door. A quick shower should wake him up enough to eat if nothing else. Stepping beneath the water a few minutes later, Adam cursed loudly at its barely lukewarm cascade. Another reason to be first out of bed he surmised quickly, soaping his body and then rinsing himself clean in what was the fastest shower he had ever taken. Which included the ones he'd taken as a boy when the water had barely touched his skin before he'd pronounced himself done. Not that he ever managed to get that one past his mother. She'd known he was going to lie before he'd even opened his mouth. His lips curved into a soft smile as he remembered the amused glint in her eye she couldn't quite hide as he assured her he'd stood under the spray for at least twenty minutes.

He sighed heavily and shut off the water before wrapping a towel around his waist and securing it firmly. Her eyes weren't lit with much of anything anymore—his father had made sure of that. Elyse

MacArthur had been a gentle soul from a ridiculously wealthy family who preferred to spend her evenings with a good book, rather than fluttering around like social butterflies in the world other debutantes of her age favored. Until young up-and- comer, Andrew Blackwell, set his sights on her—well, on her father's money.

Adam could imagine how the cripplingly shy Elyse had been swept off her feet by the dashing Blackwell, succumbing to his charm, not realizing she was merely a means to an end. Although it didn't take her long to figure it out. The wide-eyed debutante had long since disappeared beneath a sea of vodka and prescription medication to escape Andrew Blackwell's barrage of mental and verbal abuse. Being forced to bear the humiliation and scars of vicious gossip of his less than discreet affairs throughout their marriage, performing her duties as a good wife should.

He pulled on a pair of worn jeans, the fabric having softened over the years of wear and fitting him like a second skin. An image of his mother's beautiful face swam to the forefront of Adam's racing mind. If it wasn't for her, he'd have thrown off the chains of the Blackwell name long ago; but the mere thought of leaving her alone in that rambling mausoleum of a house with his father and the carbon copy of the man his brother, Michael, had become, stopped him time and time again. Which was also why, although doing his father's bidding was the last thing on earth he wanted to do, he would have to figure out how to get into Vance Wolf's office. He had no doubts that if he did not, his mother would be the one paying for his disobedience.

Adam threw on the first T-shirt he laid his hands on and then shoved his feet into the brand new pair of cowboy boots he'd bought before he left New York. He frowned at the sheen coming off them, knowing Vance Wolf would have a field day with his hasty purchase. Ignoring the rumbling of his stomach and the possibility of no breakfast, Adam walked around the room, dragging his feet and scuffing the boots on the floorboards, desperately trying to make them look as though it was *not* the first time he'd put them on.

You think he's gonna be so easily fooled?

Adam gave an inward shrug at the nudging of his inner voice. No, he didn't think it was that easy to make a fool of the ornery cowboy, but it made him feel better not to walk into the kitchen wearing boots he could see his face in. With one more scrape of the toe of his boot on the floor, Adam closed the door of his room behind him and headed for the main house.

Breakfast had been a quiet affair, filled with yawns and groans from everyone around the table. Everyone, that is, except Audrey and Vance Wolf, who were so chipper he wanted to slap the smiles off their faces. Okay, maybe not *both* of them. Now he and his four colleagues were waiting outside the barn as instructed, looking like idiots pretending to be cowboys—which is what they were. His gaze took in the little group consisting of Graham, Marcus, Phil and Nick—and of course himself. He worked alongside these guys every day, but right now he would be hard-pressed to recognize any of them. They looked like a cross between Billy Crystal, Roy Rogers and the Three Amigos. Phil's jeans actually had a perfect knife-edge crease running down the front of each leg that offered a silent challenge to anyone who dared attempt to flatten it. Graham's waistcoat had enough rhinestones on it to rival Glenn Campbell's cowboy, and Nick and Marcus—he was without words. They'd obviously been shopping at the same fancy dress store judging by their outfits, and their head wear was definitely more sombrero than Stetson.

Okay, so he looked as much of a fish out of water as they did, but at least in his T-shirt, faded jeans, newly scuffed boots and brand new Stetson, he looked a lot more cowboy than the rest of them—or he hoped he did. He grinned widely and nudged Graham who stood beside him. "You okay? You look a little green around the gills."

"Let's just say when they said never work with animals or children, they were talking about me." Graham's sheepish grin was more of a grimace. He glanced at Phil, Marcus and Nick, then down at himself and snorted. "Would you look at the state of us? We look more Glee than Gunsmoke."

Adam giggled, then he chuckled, then he belly laughed as Graham joined him. Their mirth and the reason for it was very quickly picked up on by the other three, and in moments all of them were embroiled in huge gales of laughter, alternately pointing at each other and holding onto their stomachs. And that was how Vance and Walt found them when they emerged from the barn leading the horses they were to ride. Adam caught Vance's gaze and the smile in the cowboy's eyes sent a bolt of heat through him, tightening his gut and sending delicious sparks of anticipation down his spine—until Vance cocked his eyebrow with arrogant confidence of his effect on

Adam.

Adam's grin was replaced with a scowl and his hackles rose. How big was this man's ego? Clearing his throat, Adam squared his shoulders and forced himself to meet Vance's gaze without flinching. He'd be damned if he'd give the cowboy the satisfaction of knowing how rattled he actually was. *Rattled? Is that what we're calling the urge to find out if cowboys really do it with their boots on?* Having silenced his inner voice with a two by four, Adam turned his attention to the men's dumbfounded expressions as they stared at the motley crew before them. After a few minutes Vance shook his head and let out a great belt of laughter.

"My momma will be proud of you, gentlemen, you've accomplished a first and managed to render me speechless." Vance's admission sent laughter rippling through the group again and when it subsided, he led one of the horses forward. "This is it, guys. Your first day on horseback. I hope you brought somethin' soft to sit on at dinner tonight. You're gonna need it." The tease in his voice was not malicious and the group groaned heartily in response. "The horses are well trained and are used to firm hands in the day to day job of running down the cattle. Not that I'm saying they don't appreciate a little coaxing and gentle words, but you need to show 'em who's boss or they'll take you for the ride of a lifetime and most likely throw you off at the end of it."

Everyone laughed again when Graham stated morosely, "I'm gonna die on that thing, aren't I?"

"Don't worry, big guy," Vance said with a slap to Graham's shoulder. "If Raphael makes a break for it, we'll send Phil after you. One look at those creases will stop him in his tracks."

"Hey," Phil complained. "My mom pressed these for me." The sudden blush on his cheeks at his admission had more laughter and genial arms flung around Phil's shoulders, and he batted at them good-naturedly.

Adam felt a little buzz of excitement as he chuckled with his colleagues. Although he worked with them every day, they didn't socialize outside of the office and it occurred to him how little he actually knew about them. Something he would be happy to rectify this week. He hoped he wasn't awful to work for, and that he didn't make them feel he placed himself above them, because nothing was further from the truth. In fact, when he had been promoted, he'd handpicked them from other departments because he'd been so impressed with their work. He definitely felt he had the best department in the firm, and he aimed to keep it that way.

Admittedly, he was the one who shied away from personal intrusion more than the others. He'd been invited out for drinks after work more times than he could remember, but he'd never taken them up on it. Too afraid of them finding out who he was, and that it would change their working relationship forever. How could it not? It had taken them time to get used to having a boss who was merely younger than them—what the fuck would their reaction be if they knew he was also the big boss' son? Right now, he wasn't particularly eager to find out.

"Are you with us?"

Blinking out of the thoughtful daze he had

obviously fallen into, Adam met Vance's gaze. He hadn't even heard the cowboy move to stand in front of him to offer him the reins he held. Adam looked between the long strips of leather and Vance's green eyes and back again before muttering lamely, "Sorry?"

"This is your horse, Michelangelo, Mike for short." Vance raised a questioning eyebrow. "You okay?"

Adam nodded and plucked the reins from Vance's fingers. "Yeah, I'm fine. Sorry, must have been miles away." He swallowed at the unfamiliar softness in Vance's voice as the cowboy nodded and gave him the first genuine smile Adam had seen on the man's face, the words so quiet, he had to strain to hear him.

"Glad you came back." Vance turned on his heel and Adam watched as the cowboy mounted his own horse with a grace and fluidity he would not have thought the man possessed. "Saddle up, ladies. Reins in hand, left foot in stirrup, grab the pommel and use your right leg to haul yourself up into the seat."

Ten minutes later, after much ribald teasing, they were all were seated. Graham received a resounding cheer from his colleagues when he managed, with a little help from a shove by Travis, to finally seat himself atop of Raphael—who had stood with surprising patience while poor Graham made his many attempts.

"Remember," Vance said loudly. "Use a firm hand, make sure they know who's boss. Especially you, Nick. Donatello likes to think he's cock of the walk, so he might try and take you off on a magical mystery tour."

Adam snorted out a laugh. "Donatello? Seriously?"

"What?" For the first time since they'd met, Adam saw the stain of blush on the cowboy's cheeks.

"Michelangelo," Adam elaborated. "Donatello, Raphael? Who's got Leonardo?"

"Phil," Vance said, albeit reluctantly, before sending Adam a mock-glare. "If Mr Prentiss is quite finished, we've got some fences to mend today, so I hope you're ready to get your hands dirty. Keep together and don't be afraid to call out if you get into any difficulty. I expect you to work, but I don't want you to kill yourself." He winked at them. "I mean, this *is* supposed to be fun, right?"

"Just be careful you don't get too close to each other," Adam called, falling into line behind Vance. "In case there are any ninja-style kicks." He couldn't help grinning widely at Vance as the cowboy looked back at him over his shoulder. "Come on," he said. "You named them after ninja turtles, there's no way I was gonna leave that alone."

Almost an hour later, they'd made it to the north end of the property without incident. Which had probably more to do with the snail's pace Vance had set, than their prowess on horseback—. Although Adam wasn't sure who was more surprised—him or Vance. He smiled to himself as they came to a stop. If he was honest, it was probably Graham, who had not only managed to stay atop Raphael, but had even coaxed the beautiful bay into a trot once or twice.

Adam's breath caught in his throat as he watched the muscles ripple in Vance's thighs as he dismounted. The smooth motion of his lithe body made the action look easy, and an unbidden image of Vance skittered across the surface of his mind. An image of naked limbs and glistening torso stretched out beneath him, his face a mask of ecstasy as Adam thrust into him with deep, hard strokes. He mentally shook his head, shattering the tableau and taking a few deep breaths before his dick made it more than obvious what directions his thoughts were taking. The last thing he needed was to be hounded on the ride back by ribald renditions of "bone on the range".

"Okay," Vance said, pushing his Stetson to the back of his head. "You can get off, ladies, we're here."

"I'm not sure I can," Graham groaned, wriggling in the saddle as Raphael shifted his weight. "Maybe I could just take a supervisory position—from up here."

"Come on, old-timer." Adam couldn't help but grin when Vance hooked an arm around Graham's waist and practically lifted him off the horse, setting him on the ground. Graham wasn't exactly a light man, but Vance lifted him with no more effort than if he were a child. "Stretch out a bit. It'll help you get your land legs back. You did good. Y'all did real good."

"So why are the fences down?" Marcus asked.

Adam glanced along the at least twenty feet of broken fencing lying on the grass. New wooden posts and a huge roll of barb-wire had been left along the fence edge, and he surmised Cory and Travis had probably dropped them off earlier, judging by the tire tracks nearby. He frowned at the way Vance visibly tensed at Marcus' question.

"Let's just say one of our neighbors would like to see this land added to his." Vance's voice was cold, ice dripping from every word.

"Are you saying they were broken on purpose?" Adam asked. "To what end?"

"Well, let me see. This here is a cattle ranch, right?" Adam nodded. "And what do you suppose is Wolf

Creek's main source of revenue?"

"Cattle?" Gordon chimed in helpfully.

"Well done, Gray," Vance said, pointing his finger at the older man. "So, what's the one thing you think would run a cattle rancher off his land faster than snot off a stick?"

"Seriously?" Adam's jaw dropped open on its hinges. "They're stealing your cattle?"

"Woo-hoo, give that man a ceegar," Vance said, tipping Adam a wink. "So, before we lose any more, we'd better get to fixing these fences, don't ya think?"

"Here."

Adam looked up from where he lay flat against the grass and found Vance standing over him with a bottle of water in his outstretched hand. He pushed himself up and took the bottle and smiled gratefully. "Thanks." He gestured to the ground beside him. "Care to join me?" Vance nodded and dropped down beside him with a groan. He lay back on his elbows, his hat pulled firmly down on his head, shielding his eyes from the hot afternoon sun.

The other men were sitting in a group about thirty feet away, eating what remained of the picnic lunch Cory had driven out to give them, and drinking bottled water. Their laughter carried on the breeze and he grinned as Phil and Nick obviously began to tease Graham. They'd spent the last four hours cutting and mending fences, and if poor Graham had been attacked by the barb-wire once, he'd been attacked a hundred times, leaving his colleagues no other choice but to rib him mercilessly.

They'd worked hard and there hadn't really been a

chance to talk to Vance about the cattle poaching going on at Wolf Creek. Which was why he'd asked Vance to join him, in the hope that he might get some information his father would deem important. Adam had received a text from his mother saying that his father was withholding her medication and the walls were closing in on her. Whether he liked it or not, he had no choice.

"I know this is none of my business," Adam began, his voice seeming over loud to his own ears as the words left his lips. "But how are you replacing the stolen cattle?"

"You're right, it's none of your business."

"I'm sorry. I didn't mean to pry." Adam made to push himself to his feet but was stayed by Vance's hand on his arm.

"Wait… it's me who should be sorry." Vance's tone was apologetic. "I guess I'm a little sensitive when it comes to the ranch." He sighed heavily and the weight of it touched Adam's heart. "My father lived for this land. This was one of his favorite places. He'd just ride out here to the north paddock and sit, for hours. Sometimes Momma would send me out to bring him back so he wouldn't miss dinner. Then he'd talk me into sittin' for a spell and before we knew it, we were both going to bed on empty stomachs." Vance chuckled softly, his gaze wistful. "I can't tell you how many times he sneaked into my room with sandwiches after Momma had gone to sleep, and we'd eat 'em together, gigglin' like teenagers and holdin' our breath at the slightest noise."

Adam smiled. "Sounds nice." And it did. Vance's experience of growing up was a million miles away from his. If you were late for dinner you didn't eat until his father said so, which could be anything from a day to a week, depending on his mood. Or, if he was feeling particularly generous, you were allowed to eat, after you were given a lash from his belt for every minute you were late.

"It was."

"What happened?"

"New owner bought the Garton place across the way after the old man died and it wasn't long before he put in an offer for Wolf Creek. When my father made it clear the place wasn't for sale, the asshole quit with the nicey-nice. The cattle started disappearing, their water bins were poisoned. Then we suddenly lost a couple of big accounts, and our credit at the feed store was refused after twenty years of doing business with them." Vance frowned; his confusion obvious as he studied Adam's face intently. "Why the hell am I tellin' *you* all this?"

"Sometimes it's easier to talk to a stranger," Adam said with a shrug, feeling like the world's biggest heel.

"Maybe… What was I sayin'?"

"Your dad."

"Right." Vance swallowed audibly. "The stress was too much for him. He had a heart attack after the barn was set afire. We lost some good horses that night. Petey, Tobias, Walter, and Geronimo, my Dad's palomino. God, he loved that mangy old cur. Momma used to say he'd have brought the damn thing into their bed if he could've. You know, I'd never seen my Dad cry before. But he cried over that horse, kneeling on the dirt in the dark." He shook his head as if to clear it of the image he'd evoked. Anyway, it looked like he was pulling through and the doctors discharged him. He had another the night before we were due to bring him home, and he didn't make it."

"I'm so sorry." Adam reached out before he knew he was even doing it and squeezed Vance's thigh. The warmth of Vance's leg started to seep into his palm. Adam looked at his hand on the soft denim for a few moments before snatching it back as though it burned. "Sorry." He repeated the apology, hating the flush of heat immediately felt in his cheeks.

"Don't mind me," Vance drawled. "You go ahead, city-boy."

There it was again. That goddamn arrogance. Adam gave a rueful shake of his head.

"I knew it wouldn't last."

"What wouldn't?"

"Just when I begin to think there's an actual person in there somewhere, your ego gets in the way."

"Ain't nothin' wrong with a little confidence." Vance's gaze narrowed and slid lasciviously over Adam's body. "I work hard, and play even harder, Prentiss. I'm no different to you. I just don't pussy-foot around when I see somethin' I want—I just take it."

"What if it doesn't want to be taken?"

Adam gulped as Vance leaned in close and said in a voice that dripped with Texas honey, "I think we both know that wouldn't be true."

Adam watched Vance walk back to the group, his fingers pulling at the crisp blade of grass around him in frustration. He had never met anyone so cock-sure of themselves—ever. Neither had he met anyone who curled his toes and melted his reserve with a glance. But for a few minutes he'd gotten a glimpse of the man behind the ego. It had been there in the way he'd talked about his father, his love for the man abundantly clear in his voice and the soft smile on his lips. Maybe Adam wasn't the only one hiding.

"Does that stuff of your Gamma's *really* work?"

The entire table chuckled along with Graham as he shifted in his seat, albeit laughter tinged with sympathetic groans of discomfort. When Vance had said their asses would be paying for their inexperience, he hadn't been kidding. Even Adam, who had spent more time in the saddle than the others had winced when he'd dismounted Mike. The spasm of the muscle in his right butt cheek had left him limping, much to the amusement of his colleagues.

Walt, Cody and Travis had showed them all how to unsaddle the horses and rub them down and put them away for the night. Although Walt had to explain to a tired Phil that out here your horse was like your car, and wouldn't you put the car in the garage at the end of the day? Phil reluctantly agreed but pointed out that his car didn't try to throw him out the window or make emergency stops he wasn't expecting. After the horses were settled, they'd wearily made their way into the ranch house, stomachs rumbling and mouths watering at the glorious smells emanating from the kitchen.

Vance carved the enormous turkey Audrey had prepared, and Adam was sure he was drooling as he waited for his plate to make its way around the table to him. Tureens in the centre of the table contained all the trimmings you'd expect with a Thanksgiving dinner, and Adam piled his plate high with yams and the creamiest mashed potato he'd ever tasted, topped with thick gravy. He'd never savored each mouthful like this before, each morsel lighting up his taste buds as though he'd not eaten for months. Maybe food tasted different when you'd actually worked for it.

"I take it the mashed potato is a hit, Adam."

Glancing up at the head of the table where Audrey sat, the only thing his food-addled brain could come up with was, "Huh?"

"You were moaning a little, dear."

Adam blushed and swiftly swallowed the aforementioned mash. "Sorry. It's good."

"You moan away, honey." Audrey smiled. "It's nice to know my cooking's appreciated."

"I've been dreaming about your cooking all day, Mz Audrey," Phil said around a mouthful of turkey. "And my butt has been dreaming of a soft cushion."

"I hope Vance wasn't too hard on ya'll." Adam grinned at the admonishing glare five feet of Audrey Wolf threw her son. Her over six feet of solid muscle, son.

"I just showed 'em how to be cowboys. Ain't that what they're here for?" Vance said, his tone mock-affronted that she could possibly suggest otherwise. "But I have to admit, I *was* pleasantly surprised today. When you showed up yesterday I thought I was in for a week of pissin' and moanin' from a bunch of suits who were worried they'd break a nail; but you did good— even if you did look like the sorriest excuse for cowboys I've ever seen when we headed out this mornin'." He looked pointedly at Phil, Nick and Marcus, drawing more laughter. "And guess what? Tomorrow you get to do it all again!" The groans echoed around the table, albeit good-naturedly.

"Don't tell me we got more fences to mend?" Marcus said, covering a yawn with his hand.

"Unfortunately, Marcus," Walt said, his tone solemn. "Mending fences around here is a daily job."

"But not one you'll have to do again," Vance said. Adam didn't miss the almost imperceptible shake of his head at Walt. "Tomorrow is gonna be all about roping cows, or calves anyway." He chuckled softly. "We'll start you on somethin' small. See if you can catch anything with a lasso." His green gaze settled on Adam for the last sentence, igniting a flame and creating all sorts of images in Adam's head of being caught in Vance's rope, at his mercy. Judging by the self-satisfied smirk on Vance's full lips, that was exactly what the bastard had intended. But when Vance dropped him a wink, Adam couldn't help but shake his head and smile ruefully. The cowboy might be full of it, but he had to give him points for persistence.

Adam's cell heralded the arrival of a text. He apologized as he pulled it out of his jeans pocket and then pressed the envelope on the screen. His stomach tightened at the sight of his father's name. It was short and sweet, a single question mark, nothing else, but the meaning was crystal clear. He quickly locked the screen and shoved it back into his pocket, turning his attention back to his dinner.

"Momma," Vance said in a whiney voice, like a disgruntled teenager. "Adam used his cell during dinner. We're not allowed to have phones at the table."

Adam met his gaze, his lips twitching at the teasing twinkle in Vance's eyes. "I'm a guest, rules don't apply to me," he couldn't resist countering.

"Now that's not strictly true, Adam," Audrey

chimed in, joining in the ruse. "But I'm turning a blind eye this time, 'cause you like my 'taters."

"I really do, ma'am," Adam said in his best imitation of a Texan accent. "They're mighty fine."

"Suck up." Vance mumbled, shoveling more yams into his mouth.

The entire table erupted, and the rest of the meal settled into an easy fare of banter, teasing and what they could expect tomorrow. After which, Phil and Adam were tasked with clearing the table, with Vance and Travis in charge of washing and drying the dishes. Adam smiled to himself as he picked up the tureen that had been filled to the brim with yams and was now empty. Audrey Wolf might look sweet and gentle, but there was no doubt in his mind who really ran the ranch, no matter what she allowed her son to think.

"I didn't think I'd enjoy this," Phil said as fell into step beside Adam on their way to the sink. "In fact, I thought it would be seven kinds of hell on earth, but I'm glad we came." He nudged Adam with his shoulder. "It's good to see you without that stick up your ass."

Adam's eyes widened at that and he put the crockery he carried onto the kitchen counter. "Stick up my ass?" he echoed. "Is that how you all see me? I thought I was an okay boss."

"You are, you are," Phil quickly reassured him. "Don't get me wrong. It's just we only know that side of you. Even though we've worked together for a long time, we've only really ever met Adam Prentiss... not Adam."

Adam nodded in agreement. He'd often thought the same himself, so it wasn't exactly as though Phil was talking out of turn. "And is he okay? Adam, I mean."

Phil grinned from ear to ear and shoved Adam playfully. "They both are, man. They both are. Now shut up before the swelling music starts to play and I have to get the tissues out—and everybody knows cowboys don't cry."

"Okay, Roy Rogers," Adam said, letting out a bark of laughter. "But considering the way your eyes were watering when you hit the ground this afternoon, I think we both know that ain't true." He gathered the last of the plates from the table and strode back across the kitchen to the sink where Vance was now elbow deep in soap suds.

"You and Phil seem to be having fun."

Adam shrugged, setting the plates down on the counter. "I didn't realize they saw me as just their boss. Maybe this week wasn't such a bad idea after all."

"My thoughts precisely."

Adam was about to respond when his cell chirped in his pocket. Obviously, he knew who it was going to be without looking at it. His father didn't like to be ignored. "Excuse me," he tried to keep his voice as casual as he could. "Work stuff."

Vance lifted his chin in acknowledgement and Adam could feel his eyes burning into his skin as he walked away. Once he was out of the kitchen, Adam yanked his cell from his pocket and opened the text.

Your mother's looking a little pale.

Adam sighed heavily, his mother's face skating across the surface of his mind. Squaring his shoulders, he looked around him to get his bearings. Not that he knew the layout of the house that well, but there had to be an office somewhere. He glanced over his shoulder to double-check he was still alone, and then headed down the long hall to the back of the house. Three corridors came off the hallway and he trotted down the first one, but only found two bedrooms and a family sized bathroom. In the second corridor the first two doors opened up onto a store cupboard and a huge bedroom, but the third yielded the treasure he was hoping for—a desk and wall to wall filing cabinets. He looked behind him one more time and then slipped inside the room, pulling the door to behind him.

Gazing around the room Adam took in the masculine decor of deep Mexican reds complimenting the dark wood of the floor and the furniture. This was definitely a man's room. *For God's sake, Adam,* he admonished himself. *Get on with it, you can ask him who does his decorating later.* He crossed the room to the huge desk, the top of which could barely be seen beneath the paperwork strewn across it. Adam tried not to disturb the reams of paper too much as he sifted through them, looking for anything that would shed some light as to the ranch's financial position.

Ten minutes later, on the verge of giving up, Adam's fingers touched a thick, leather bound book. He pulled it from its hiding place under the pile of papers. His stomach tightened in anticipation—an accounts ledger. Adam opened it and flicked through the pages. The beginning of the year had started out strong for Wolf Creek and their profits were growing, but then they began to take a nosedive about nine months ago when— Adam couldn't believe what he was seeing.

New neighbor came by. Bought the old Garton place across the way. Some businessman out of state. Says his name's Andrew Blackwell.

What? His father owned the neighboring ranch? When? How? His father was the one breaking fences and stealing cows and poisoning waterholes and burning down barns? Adam's head began to spin. *What the fuck was going on here?*

The words gave way to everyday figures about the running of the ranch, then his father's name showed up again and again.

More cattle missing from south paddock. Spoke to sheriff, he said he'd look into it.

Actually caught some men poaching cattle off our land. Called Sheriff Fucknuts, who said there were no cattle on the truck so we couldn't prove intent. Bet Blackwell is laughing his ass off.

Losing money hand over fist. Been working with Rusty's feed store for over twenty years... credit was refused this morning when Vance went to pick up our order. Really worried, hate lying to Vance and Audrey, but we're going down. Blackwell might get his hands on this place after all.

Then six months ago the writing was in a fresh hand.

Dad's gone. Blackwell is gonna pay for hounding my father into an early grave—if it's the last thing I do.

"Looking for something?"

Adam's blood ran cold through his veins. His stomach gave a nauseous lurch, his heart lodged in his throat. Vance's voice held an edge of steel Adam had never heard before and it sent a shiver up his spine. He swallowed hard and slowly turned to face him, the open ledger still in his hands. Vance leaned against the door jamb, his stance one of nonchalance, his arms crossed, and sardonic eyebrow cocked in question—although the bristling tension in his body and the intensity of his glare belied the casual pose.

Shit!

With a mouth as dry as the Sahara, Adam fought to force the words past his lips. "Hey. I got turned around." He huffed out a pathetic excuse for a laugh. "This place is like a maze and it doesn't take much to get lost."

Vance's gaze narrowed and flitted to the ledger in Adam's hands. "And you thought you'd have a look at the books while you were here?"

"God, *no*." Adam dropped the book as though it burned his fingers and it hit the desk with a thud, giving him a few seconds to come up with a plausible answer.

Oh, this should be good.

The dry bark of laughter from his inner voice did nothing to steel his resolve and Adam wanted to kick himself for the lame explanation that fell from his own tongue. "It was on the floor. I was just picking it up." He swallowed; certain the man could hear it from across the room. He waited for Vance to stride towards him, grab him by the collar and demand answers. But he didn't, which was somehow more unnerving. Vance continued to lean against the doorway, his green gaze narrowed intently on Adam. The silence stretched between them until Adam couldn't stand it any longer. He strode purposefully toward the door, and Vance. There was no option left to him other than to stop in front of the cowboy and wait for him to move. A fist tightened in Adam's gut as Vance pushed himself up straight, placed his hands against the door jambs and blocked his way even more effectively. He hated the crack in his voice, but he'd worry about that later. Right now, getting out of this room without Vance realizing what he was doing was his only concern. "Sorry. I'll get out of your way." He force a chuckle. "But you'll have to get out of mine first."

"Do you think I'm stupid, Prentiss?"

"What?"

"Do you think I don't know what you're *really* doing in here?"

"What are you talking about?" Adam stepped back as Vance took a step forward. "I told you. I got turned around."

"Ah," Vance said, continuing to approach, guiding Adam back toward the desk, without a single touch. His deep green eyes darkened as he closed the gap between them. "You got "turned around" and ended up in the one room you were likely to find me." It wasn't a question and a heat burned low in his belly in response to that in Vance's gaze. "Rather convenient, don't you think?"

"Convenient?" Adam frowned, starting as his ass hit the edge of the desk. What was the man going on about? Being caught red-handed with the ledger in his hand was far from his definition of convenient. He gasped at the sudden press of Vance's body against his. Hands either side of him, palms flat on the desktop, hemming him in. Adam swallowed hard. The heat of Vance's skin burned into his through his T-shirt, the cowboy's breath warm on his cheek.

"If you wanted to get me alone, all you had to do was ask." Vance's voice oozed sultry promise.

At least your cover's not blown. Although I get the feeling it ain't your cover he wants to blow.

Adam shot his inner voice a kick to the nuts and

stared in incredulous amazement at Vance, the effect of the man's nearness quickly pushed aside. He pushed at the arrogant bastard's shoulders, huffing out a derisive laugh, shoving him hard. The force making Vance step back to regain his balance. "Are *all* Texans full of it, or is it just you?" This time it was Vance stepping back as Adam advanced. "Sorry to burst your bubble, cowboy, but you're not as irresistible as you think."

Adam shouldered his way past Vance, wanting to get out of the room as quick as possible. The breath caught in his throat when Vance grabbed Adam's forearm and hauled him against his rock hard torso.

"You sure about that?"

There was no time to form a response before Vance's lips covered his in a breath-stealing kiss. The scratch of Vance's stubble against his skin sent sparks of heat straight to Adam's cock now pressing against the confines of his jeans. He wasn't even sure he could call it a kiss. The merging of their mouths was more of a full on assault by Vance, who took immediate control, giving Adam little choice but to open up to the insistent demand of his tongue. The way Vance kissed him was filled with an intensity the likes of which he'd never felt before—and he felt it *everywhere*. Vance's hands slid over the curve of his ass and pulled Adam impossibly closer, leaving him in no doubt of the effect he had on him. The hard length of the cowboy's shaft pressed against his thigh. Of their own volition, Adam's hands crept up Vance's chest and into his hair. The soft strands against Adam's fingers like a dash of cold water to his senses.

Adam pushed hard at Vance's shoulders, breaking the kiss. He stared down at Vance where he had landed on the floor. He wanted to slap the confusion off Vance's face. The jerk actually had the nerve to look at him as though he couldn't believe Adam hadn't fallen at his feet. Adam threw his arms out to the sides in frustration.

"What is wrong with you? Do I have fuck me tattooed on my forehead?"

"You weren't exactly fighting me off!" Vance yelled, getting to his feet and glaring just as coldly back at Adam.

Adam was furious. Mostly because Vance was right. He hadn't fought him off—hadn't wanted to. In fact, it was all he could do not to throw himself back into Vance's arms and give himself over to whatever he wanted to do to him—and probably beg for more—but he wouldn't.

"You've been sending me signals all day," Vance growled. "So, the question should be, what the hell is wrong with *you*?"

"You're deluded," Adam said, scrubbing a hand through his hair in frustration. "If I wanted you there wouldn't be a need for signals. You'd already be bent over that desk with your pants around your ankles."

"I don't think so, city-boy," Vance said, the scoff clear in his voice. "Vance Wolf don't bend over for *any* man."

"Vance Wolf? Third person? Really?" Adam sneered sarcastically. "You do know that's you, right?"

"Yeah, I know it's me." Vance said, crossing his arms. "*And* I know what I want, and I ain't too chicken shit to admit it. Which brings us to an even more intriguing question. What are you scared of, Prentiss?"

"*Please*," Adam said, bristling. "Don't try and

psycho-analyze me, *Wolf.* You don't *know* me." Vance took a step forward and Adam retreated instinctively. If Vance got close enough to touch him, his resolve would crumble. Why the hell did his father send him here? What was so special about *this* piece of land? If he gave in to the attraction between them, would it be because *he* wanted it, or because it was what his father commanded? He swallowed hard as Vance dropped his hands to his sides and curled them into frustrated fists.

"No, I don't. But I'd like to."

"No, you wouldn't." Adam shook his head. "You just want an ass to fuck, it doesn't have to be mine."

"Now who's psycho-analyzing? You don't know *me* either."

"No, I don't, and I don't want to." Snapping his mouth shut, Adam turned on his heel. Then walked sedately from the room, doing his utmost to keep his steps even and controlled—when all he wanted to do was run.

Chapter five

Vance couldn't sleep. He'd given up telling himself it was the heat about two hours ago and admitted it had more to do with intense grey eyes and soft lips than the particularly humid nights they'd been having. He couldn't figure this guy out. All the signs were there. Hell, you couldn't fake the kind of want he'd seen in Adam's eyes, yet he was pushing him away—literally. But that kiss. *God,* that kiss. Adam had got his back up and he'd meant it to be hard and fast, an 'I told you so' kind of kiss; but it had turned into something more— much more.

Closing his eyes, Vance slid his hand down his body and palmed his rapidly hardening dick through his boxers. The moment Adam's lips had met his, any attempt at the kiss remaining perfunctory was immediately forgotten. Adam's mouth had been soft and compliant beneath his, and he'd tasted of the apple pie they'd had for dessert. A deliciously heady mix of soft and sweet. Not what he was usually attracted to at all. Most of his hook-ups were hard-assed cowboys, muscled, furry and passing through. Not lean, slim-hipped pretty boys who were more at home behind a computer than in the saddle. But that city-boy—there was something about that city-boy that heated his blood and made him want to hold him in his arms and chase away the shadows he'd seen in Adam's eyes.

His fingers dipped beneath the waistband of his shorts and curled around his engorged shaft. Vance moaned softly on a hiss of breath. The warmth of his palm on his heated flesh sent sparks of pleasure to his nerve endings. He reluctantly pulled his hand out of his shorts. His dick almost screamed in frustration, but he needed something a little more tonight.

Vance pulled open the bottom drawer of his nightstand and scrabbled around until he found the smooth rounded tip of his masturbator. He took it out and dropped it on the bed beside him, then grabbed the lube. His dick was throbbing with the anticipation of sliding into the tight makeshift hole of the toy. And his mind throbbed with the images of Adam stretched out, naked and wanting, begging to be taken.

A groan pushed its way up his throat and he swallowed hard. The cap of the lube flipped open with the slightest of pressure from his thumb. Vance's lips twitched as he briefly wondered if the ease of opening meant he'd been jerking off a little excessively of late. Right now, he didn't care. He squirted a liberal amount of lubricant into the palm of his hand and held his breath as he rubbed it over his dick. The breath he'd been holding whistled through his lips at the first touch of the cool gel on his hot flesh. His hips arched off the bed as he coated himself, desperately seeking some much needed friction. There would be no perfunctory stroking tonight, he wanted to live out his fantasy *right-the-fuck-now!*

Vance picked up the masturbator and smeared some of the lube around the entrance with the head of his dick. He was so sensitive he was concerned he wouldn't last long enough to use the damn thing. The warm, skin-like sleeve stretched and then closed around him as he pushed into it. God it felt so good, so real. Okay, maybe not *real* but was sure as hell close enough. He let his eyes drift shut.

Adam's face didn't take long to form behind his closed lids. Smokey gray eyes darkened by desire. The short strands of his hair ruffled by Vance's fingers. Those full, pouty lips parted on a sigh, tongue moistening the lower. Vance cursed under his breath. Breath that fell from his lips in short, sharp gasps. Hips driving into the channel, meeting every downward pump of his wrist.

Fuck! Fuck! He shouted out his pleasure, but not a word fell from his lips. Having his bedroom two doors away from his parents' had taught him to keep certain aspects of life quiet. He was losing control. His orgasm tingled in his spine, needing just a little more before it engulfed him. He imagined Adam's peach of an ass in his hands, bouncing on his cock, head thrown back in ecstasy, hot streams of white pumping from his dick while Vance pounded into him. The moment that image became a thought it was all over.

Vance stiffened and exploded inside the masturbator, the warmth of his seed on his skin a sensation he couldn't even begin to describe. His orgasm flowed through him. Every muscle twitching in time with his racing heart. Finally, he stilled, and eased the toy off his still half-hard dick. He quickly pushed the skin-like sheath into the smooth black container and dropped it on top of the pile of clothes by the bed. He'd clean it in the morning. Right now, he didn't even have the basic motor functions to put his dick back in his pants. The intricate cleaning of sex toys needed to be attempted when his blood had made its way back up North to his brain.

Reaching down the side of the bed, he picked up the shirt he'd worn earlier. He cleaned himself of stray splashes of semen and lube, then tossed it back to the floor. Settling against the pillows, Vance sighed heavily. His orgasm may have been intense, but it didn't really live up to holding Adam in his arms.

Vance lifted his head and thumped the pillow. When he was satisfied, he'd beaten the thing into submission, he threw himself, face down, onto it. *Hold him in his arms?* What the fuck was wrong with him? The only thing he wanted to hold onto was this land. Wolf Creek was the reason for everything. He'd never had the time nor the inclination to hold onto anyone longer than it took to shoot his load. Simple and uncomplicated, exactly how he liked it. Vance sighed heavily and closed his eyes. If that were true, why did he have this deep-seated ache to have his arms wrapped around more than the pillow?

"Come on, Wolf! Get your ass outta bed or you'll be riding out on an empty stomach!"

What the fuck? Prentiss? Vance opened a bleary eye and squinted at the liquid crystal display of his clock radio. No, he hadn't—couldn't have—could he? He opened the other eye and swore loudly. Yes—he had! He'd slept through the fuckin' alarm for the first time since he was a teenager. Vance threw off the duvet and jumped out of bed, stubbing his toe on the nightstand.

"Jesus fuckin' Christ!" he cursed again and grabbed his toe, hopping around his bedroom on one foot. He heard Adam snigger from the other side of the door and his gaze narrowed. *Yeah, you laugh it up city-boy.* A sly grin lifted his lips as the words he'd yelled to hurry up Adam yesterday were thrown back at him.

"Do you need help fixing your hair?"

Vance stood up and crossed the room, stepping out of his shorts on the way. He opened the door and stared straight into Adam's eyes, noting with satisfaction the way the man's gaze dropped to his cock, heavy against his thigh. "I can manage the hair, but there's a spot behind my balls I can never quite reach if you're offerin'."

Adam's cheeks flushed with embarrassment, but he seemed to be waging a battle of his own behind those gray eyes. Vance's breath caught in his throat as Adam's tongue snaked out to moisten his lips and he took a step into the room. Anticipation caused goose bumps to break out on Vance's skin. His cock took a definite interest in proceedings, twitching against his thigh. *He's not—is he?* Adam reached out slowly, his gaze never leaving Vance's and… yanked the door out of Vance's hand, slamming it shut. He listened to Adam's retreating footsteps and stared at the white-painted wood, open-mouthed. *Son of a bitch.* Then he smiled. Then he began to chuckle. Then he laughed so hard his face hurt and his ribs ached. Man, he was liking Adam Prentiss more every minute.

Ten minutes later Vance all but threw himself into the chair opposite Adam at the kitchen table. His shower may have only been what his mother liked to call a 'spit and polish', but there was no way he was going to give Adam the no end of amusement it would provide if Vance missed breakfast. He caught Adam's eye as he reached for the bacon and dropped him a wink, unable to keep the smirk off his face when Adam blushed—somewhat predictably. If he was honest, that faint red stain on Adam's cheeks was one of the things about the man he found so fascinating. How could Adam hold his own in a boardroom without batting an eye, but one glance had him blushing like a virgin on her wedding night? Vance's smirk turned into a grin as he piled his plate high with sausage, bacon and eggs. Adam Prentiss could deny their attraction all he wanted—but that flush called him a liar.

"Are we really going to rope cows today, Vance?"

Vance nodded and mumbled around a forkful of eggs, "Sure are, Phil."

"*Big* cows?" Phil ventured.

After slowly chewing his mouthful to increase the tension, Vance swallowed before answering. He gazed solemnly at Phil and said in a low, menacing tone, "The biggest." Unable to hold his control at the look of pure terror on Phil's face, Vance cracked, and a resounding guffaw echoed around the room.

"You bastard," Phil said, good-naturedly, realizing he'd been played.

"Don't you worry, Phil," Walt chuckled. "You can go home with stories of how you rode down a cow, lassoed, roped and tied it. Just don't tell anyone how small the cow was. It'll be our little secret. What happens on the ranch stays on the ranch."

"Yep," Vance shoved more food into his mouth, and received a disapproving glare from Audrey as he sprayed half of it over the table when he spoke. "Just like Vegas. So, if you and Raphael decide you want to take your relationship to the next level, we can arrange that for you."

The table erupted and Phil was at the mercy of the other men's ribbing. Although from the look on Graham's face, Vance could see the older man was glad the heat was off himself after yesterday's riding lesson. He picked up his cup and slurped at his coffee, swallowing the now lukewarm liquid down before slamming the cup onto the table. "Come on, clear your plates, we've got cows waiting on us." He grinned at Phil. "Little ones."

Vance felt a nudge to his booted foot from beneath the table and he glanced up at Adam, since his was the direction it came. Adam's lips were curled in a soft smile and his eyes were alight with the laughter they'd all shared, but there was something else. A flicker so brief he wasn't completely sure it had been there at all. But it had… it had. For a fleeting moment Adam had smiled at him with open affection before the shutters slammed down. Vance watched as Adam blinked, obviously suddenly aware Vance had seen too much, and dropped his gaze. He watched Adam stand up, gather his plates and carry them over to the counter. City-boy was hiding something, and he was going to find out—today.

"Okay, ladies." Vance grinned at the motley crew standing against the fence, ropes in hand, awaiting his instructions. Motley they might be, but they looked a lot more like cowboys today in their T-shirts and jeans than they had yesterday. Although Nick had refused to swap his mini-sombrero for a Stetson. While the breakfast things had been cleared away, Cory and Travis had set up the six bales of hay with horns attached at one end and a tail at the other. One sat in front of Vance and the others were spaced out in front of the 'ladies'. "What we're gonna do today is learn everything you need to know about a rope." He scoffed at Phil's slack-jawed look and shook his head. "Did you seriously think I'd let you near my herd with those creases? I thought this was a much safer option, for you and the cows."

After another ripple of laughter had settled down, he showed them the rope he held in his hand. "This is the boring bit. But if you don't know the rope, the only thing you'll be tying up is yourself," his gaze flitted to Adam, and he lowered his voice purposefully, "or someone else." Adam glared at him for a few moments, but the glare soon gave way to a twitch of the lips, followed by a full on smile as the man slowly shook his head. If nothing else, Vance was certain his outright nerve was starting to hammer a chink in Adam's armor.

Twenty minutes later after a sermon on the integral parts of the rope—including the Hondo, the correct length of the shank, size of the lasso and how to make a decent coil—the men were attempting to rope their makeshift cows. And Vance was trying very hard not to cry with laughter. His stomach was in knots and his ribs ached as he watched Nick and Marcus tangle themselves in each other's ropes. They'd managed to lasso everything *but* the horns sticking out of the bale of hay. He was beginning to think that if he let them loose on the range, there'd be a lot of uprooted bushes and fence posts all over Wolf Creek.

"I got it!"

Vance cheered along with everyone else when Graham managed to get the lasso around the horns of his bale and then wrapped his arms around his stomach when Graham yanked too hard on the shank and made his cow do a back flip. He clapped Graham on the back. "You're a natural, Gray," he chuckled. "A complete natural." He glanced over at Adam who was still having trouble getting the coil right, never mind actually throwing the rope. Kicking up the dirt as he walked along the line, Vance stopped behind Adam and crossed his arms. If he was more of a gentleman, he'd probably not have stared quite so intently at the curve of Adam's ass. But as he'd never professed to being anything other than Texas cowboy through and through, he figured it was okay to gaze at that peach a little longer before making his presence known. He couldn't help but smile when Adam almost jumped three feet in the air at the loud clearing of Vance's throat. "You okay there, City-boy?" He tried to keep the laughter from his voice as Adam's obvious frustration with the rope escalated.

"I can't get the stupid fucking thing to coil." Adam's response was ground out through gritted teeth. "I'm doing exactly what you said."

"No, you're not."

"*Yes*, I am."

"*No*, you're not." Vance's gaze widened as Adam spun around and threw the rope at him. It bounced off Vance's chest and landed on the ground at his feet.

"You do it then!"

"Un-bunch your sequined chaps, Hop-a-long Cassidy," Vance said, unable to resist the tease at the thunderous expression on Adam's face. He bent and picked up the rope and tucked it under his arm. Then he put his hand on Adam's shoulder and turned him so that

Adam's back was toward him. "Stand still," he said when Adam mumbled something under his breath and tried to turn back. "Do you want to learn how to do this, or not?"

"Stop shoving me," Adam said, harrumphing loudly as he returned to the position Vance had put him in.

"Quit your yappin'," Vance countered, his grin widened at the tension in Adam's shoulders. Vance closed the gap between them and slid his arms through Adam's, held out the rope and indicated Adam should take the end of the rope in his hand. He curled his fingers around Adam's and rested his chin on Adam's shoulder so he could see the rope. Well, he had to, didn't he? Adam wasn't *that* much shorter than him and it made sense…, right? Although Adam's scent, a heady mix of the sandalwood notes of his cologne and sweat was extremely distracting, he was sure he could cope. "Now, pay attention."

"What do you think you're doing?" Adam's voice was low enough so no one else could hear.

"Teaching you how to coil a rope."

"Is that what they call sexual harassment out here?" Adam replied conversationally.

"Sexual harassment?" Vance laughed and said softly, "Trust me, *City-boy*. If you were being sexually harassed, you'd know it." He felt Adam shudder against him and couldn't help the twinge of satisfaction. "Now, shut up and pay attention.

"Keep your left hand tight on the rope, and with your right hand, you want to slide along until you have a piece roughly an arms length, that way, you'll get a decent coil. If it's shorter it won't flip and if it's longer, it'll just get messy and you'll be tripping over the damn thing."

"I did that," Adam grumbled. "The rope must be faulty."

"*Seriously?*" Vance shot Adam a derisive look. "That's what you're going with? A faulty rope?"

"Shut up and get on with it."

"Well I ain't doing all the work," Vance said, nudging Adam with his shoulder. "Get an arm's length of rope, that's it. Now turn the rope over." He frowned as Adam kind of waved the rope. "What are you doing? You need to turn it, don't just put it in your hand, it won't coil. Keep your wrist relaxed, flip it over and put it into your left hand." Vance tutted in amazement. "Just *flip* it." He lowered his voice. "I *know* for a fact your wrist is limper than that, Prentiss. Flip the goddamn rope." That comment earned him a hard heel to the toe of his boot, and he swore under his breath. "Which part of 'turn the rope over' are you not gettin'?"

"I told you," Adam muttered. "There's something wrong with—"

"If you say it's the rope one more time, I'm gonna tie you to an anthill with it—naked."

"Stop pushing me," Adam ground out.

"Just grow a pair and flip the goddamn rope." Vance couldn't understand it. He could feel Adam shaking against him. What the hell was going on? It was just a rope for Pete's sake. "Come—" He was cut off as Adam struggled free from his arms and then shoved him, sending Vance teetering backward and into the corral fence.

"I said *stop pushing*!"

Vance watched in stunned amazement, along with the rest of the group, as Adam stomped off in the direction of the bunkhouse. He stared after Adam for a few moments and then cleared his throat and turned to the other men. "Well, ladies, it looks like the boss man is takin' a break. Come on, don't just stand there, get those ropes a-spinning, we got cows to catch." *What the hell just happened?*

Chapter six

Adam threw himself on the mattress and stared up at the ceiling. His breath fell in harsh gasps from between parted lips and his heart banged against his ribcage. It had been so long ago. He'd thought he'd gotten over it. His body shook from head to toe and the room seemed to spin around him. Over it, huh? Apparently not. He sat up and ran his shaking hands through his hair, gripping at the strands. Maybe if he put his head between his knees or something—

Adam looked up as the door swung open, Vance stepped into the room and kicked it closed behind him. *What now?* "Please," he mumbled, dropping his head into his hands. "Just leave me alone."

"I don't think so, Prentiss," Vance replied. "Have you seen you? You're as white as a sheet. What the hell happened out there?"

"God! What is gonna take? An anvil with the word Acme written on the side of it falling from the sky and landing on your head? Take the hint. *Go away.*" Adam felt the mattress sink beside him and he shook his head in disbelief. Then wished he hadn't because the room lurched ominously. "You just don't quit, do you." It wasn't a question. "You're like a dog with a bone. A really *big* bone." An open bottle of water was pushed into his hand.

"Sip this." Vance's tone brooked no argument.

The ice cold water slid across his tongue and Adam swilled it around his mouth before swallowing. "Thanks," he murmured, handing the bottle back to Vance. He flinched at Vance's fingers warm on the back of his neck, startled. "Haven't you groped me enough for one day?"

"Shut up," Vance drawled, the derision clear. "Close your eyes and focus on me kneading your skin. Take some deep breaths. In through your nose for the count of seven and out through your mouth for eleven. You need to calm down, man. Your pulse is going nuts and I know it ain't *all* me."

If his heart didn't feel as though it were about to jump out of his chest, Adam was sure he could have come back with a suitable rejoinder. But right now, for the first time since he'd met Vance, he was going to do as he was told. He knew it was a panic attack. Knew it was up to him to get it under control, so he did as he was bid and closed his eyes.

It took him a while, but eventually, concentrating on the gentle rub of Vance's fingers against the nape of his neck, Adam's breathing evened out and his pulse returned to normal, and the world straightened on its axis. Vance removed his hand and gave him the water again, instructing him to take a swig.

"Better?" Vance asked, his green eyes the last thing Adam expected to see, concerned.

"Yeah, thanks."

"Good. Now talk," Vance said, insistently. "What happened? Was it me?"

"*No.*" Adam shook his head, glad the room didn't tip this time.

"Look," Vance gazed into his eyes. "There's something going on here between us. I know it and you know it—no matter how much you try to deny it." He brushed Adam's hair back from his forehead with an unexpected tenderness. "But you need to know something. I would *never* cross the line."

Adam stared at him, noting the sincerity in his eyes. Of course, he knew that. But to hear Vance say it out loud warmed his heart. For all his brash cowboy bravado, Adam instinctively knew Vance was not the type of man who would hurt another person on purpose.

"If it wasn't me," Vance said softly. "What was it?"

Adam shrugged and took another long draw from the bottle. "It was the rope."

"The rope?" Vance shook his head, confused. "'Cause you couldn't make it coil?"

"No." Adam swallowed hard. "The feel of it. The touch of it on my skin." He glanced at Vance and sighed. "You're not going to let it go at that, are you?"

"Nope," Vance replied solemnly. "Adam, if there's something going on I should know, you need to tell me. What if there are other things around the ranch that could set off a panic attack like the one you just had? I ought to know so I can be prepared if it happens again."

Annoyingly, Vance was right. But Adam didn't want to tell him. Didn't want to open himself up to such vulnerability. Not twice in one day. "Well," he mumbled. "Unless you've got a boa constrictor hidden in the barn, I think we're okay."

Vance chuckled softly. "Not a fan of snakes, huh?" Adam half-grinned in response. "I guess if you add the rope thing to the snakes, your alternative career is as a snake-charmer is kind of a no go."

"Cute," Adam said, unable to hold back a snort of laughter. "You should be on the stage. The cowboy comedian." He groaned loudly. The bastard was still waiting for an answer. Adam took a deep breath. "Alright, alright. It was the rope. When I was a kid, if I missed my chores, or mouthed-off, or didn't clear my plate, my dad used to tie me to the chair and leave me there until he considered I was suitably contrite." He gazed at his hands. "Sometimes it was for hours at a time with no food, no water, no bathroom breaks. There were times when he forgot, and I'd be left alone, in the dark."

"Adam—"

"Anyway," Adam said, and downed the rest of the water before he put the bottle on the nightstand. "That's it. No big deal."

"No big *deal?*" Vance's voice was low and menacing. Adam stared at him, noting the high points of color in his cheeks and the firm set of his mouth. "Are you fuckin' kidding me? You don't do that to a kid. You must have been terrified."

"To be honest, I thought I was over it." Adam scrubbed a hand over his face. "I made an idiot of myself."

"No, you didn't." Adam raised an eyebrow and Vance's lips twitched in response. "Okay, maybe a bit. But let's face it, Phil's still winning in the idiot stakes with those jeans."

Adam chuckled, the first genuine chuckle he'd uttered since he was handed the rope earlier. "I think they should be bronzed."

Vance let out a bellow of laughter. "The blacksmith

owes me a favor or two, maybe he can rustle something up."

Adam watched Vance's face light up as he laughed and the desire to feel that wide, soft mouth on his was overwhelming. He tried to drag his gaze from Vance's lips—honest—but it seemed an impossible task. What was he doing? What happened to the 'avoid him like the plague' idea? He couldn't allow his personal feelings to get in the way of why he was here. His mother was depending on him. But the memory of Vance's searing kiss—*God.* He wanted to feel it again.

His lips parted on a sigh as Vance's gaze dropped to his mouth. He obviously wasn't the only one thinking about the last time they'd been alone. The silence stretched between them for what seemed like forever, until Adam couldn't stand the anticipation a moment longer. "Fuck it," he mumbled; closed the gap between them and pressed his lips to Vance's.

Vance's mouth opened immediately beneath the pressure of Adam's and he took complete control of the kiss, propelling Adam back onto the pillows with the weight of his muscled frame. Adam groaned low in his throat and carded his fingers through Vance's thick hair, loving the soft feel of the heavy strands against his skin as Vance ravaged his mouth. His dick hardened at the rub of Vance's thigh and he involuntarily lifted his hips, searching for a heavier touch.

Being kissed by Vance could only be likened to a full scale attack on the senses. Every nerve-ending in Adam's body felt as though they were the strings of a harp, plucked by a master, humming with need. Vance mapped out every ridge and curve on the roof of Adam's mouth, then slid his tongue sensuously against

Adam's, drawing him into a sensual dance he never wanted to end. When Vance's fingers slipped beneath the hem of his T-shirt and splayed across the slightly soft mound of his belly, Adam wrenched his lips from Vance's, gasping for air. Gazing into Vance's eyes, sharing the same breath, the cowboys touch burned into his skin, two words bounced around his skull in huge neon lights—*need him*— The heavy knock on Adam's door broke them apart, sending them scrabbling for opposite ends of the bed while shaking fingers straightened disheveled clothing.

"Vance? You in there?" It was Walt.

"Yeah," Vance's voice was remarkably calm. Adam was impressed. "What is it, Walt?" Adam's breath caught in his throat and Vance visibly stiffened when Walt rasped a single word through the closed door.

"Midnight."

Vance all but flew off the bed and crossed the room in two strides, the door creaking ominously as he yanked it open. He stared at his foreman for a few seconds and then began to bark out orders. The first of which was to call the vet. Adam didn't say a word, merely got up and followed the two men from the room. For all his tough exterior, Midnight meant a lot to him and, although he didn't know how much, if any, help he would be; he did know he wanted to be there— for Vance. He'd worry about the why of that statement later.

Inside the barn, he followed Vance into Midnight's stall and stood in the corner, out of the way. The horse paced restlessly, and Adam could see the sheen of sweat on her coat. He watched in silence as Vance murmured soothing noises on his approach toward her.

The connection between man and beast had been obvious before—but now—Adam's gut tightened. The plea in her soft brown eyes was almost unbearable as she nuzzled her face into Vance's solid chest.

"Hey there, pretty girl," Vance said softly, his fingers gentle on her velvety nose. "This is it. We're finally gonna get to meet that little one you've been cooking up." He sighed heavily, resting his forehead against her muzzle. "I know you're scared, but you can do this. And I'll be right here with you, every step of the way. So, you just do your thing, Momma, and I'll be here if you need me."

Adam's mouth parted in surprise as Midnight nudged him one more time with her nose and then returned to her pacing. If he didn't know better, he'd have sworn she understood every word Vance had said. He took a moment to study Vance's face as the cowboy walked toward him. It was the first time he'd ever seen fear in those cool green eyes. Albeit only for a moment—but he'd seen it.

"Lunch'll probably be ready in a minute," Vance said, gruff nonchalance in his voice. "This could take hours. You don't have to wait."

"I know," Adam replied simply, not moving. Vance stared at him intently for a few moments, then left the stall, returning almost immediately with two wooden stools. He closed the door and put the stools on the floor in the corner, making sure they were out of Midnight's way.

"Make yourself comfortable."

Adam sat down on the stool next to Vance and they watched Midnight wander up and down her stall. While they sat there in a companionable silence, Adam became intrigued at how the horse prepared herself for the new arrival. How her body took over and she was no longer the master of her own fate, but now running on a base instinct as old as time itself. He leaned against the wall and crossed his arms, the warmth of Vance's thigh against his as they settled down to wait.

Vance fumbled with the belt holding up Adam's jeans. "I'm gonna make you feel so good, baby. Make you scream for me."

Unable to contain the moans low in his throat, Adam delved his fingers into Vance's unruly red-brown hair and gripped tightly in anticipation. His knees trembled as Vance dropped to the hay-strewn floor before him. "Do it, just do—"

"Adam?"

Adam's eyes flew open at the bellow of his name and stared around him vacantly. Yep—they were still in Midnight's stall—but Vance was gently rubbing Midnight down, not on his knees in the hay moistening sinfully soft lips. He'd been dreaming—*fuck!* Unfortunately, his dick wasn't as quick to catch on as his brain. His engorged flesh pressed painfully against its denim restriction and Adam pulled his jacket down further, hoping to cover up the evidence.

"What?" he croaked; his throat thick with sleep. "Did I miss it?"

"Not yet." Vance chuckled, not faltering in his steady stroking rhythm along Midnight's neck. He tilted his head in question. "You were dreamin' and, from the sounds of it, you were havin' a *real* good time. What were you dreamin' about?"

"I don't know, can't remember." Adam shrugged

and reached down beside him for the flask of coffee he'd popped into the house for earlier, to keep them both awake. He unscrewed the top and took a healthy swig—then winced. It was cold and grainy. He swallowed the bitter grounds and then wiped at his tongue with a gloved hand, much to Vance's amusement. "What time is it?" He lost the last couple of words in a huge yawn that cracked his jaw.

"Almost nine-thirty," Vance said. The fact that he didn't look at his watch told Adam he'd already checked the time recently.

Adam stood up and stretched, lifting his arms high over his head and bending to the side. His back creaked at the movement, but it unknotted his muscles, so he ignored the complaint. He walked over to Midnight and stroked her velvety nose. "Hey, beautiful. How're you doing?"

"I called the vet again," Vance said softly. "Somethin' doesn't feel right."

"What do you mean?" Adam looked Midnight over. She looked the same as she had two hours ago when Vance had explained to him the three different stages of equine labor. "Her water didn't even break ye—" He yelped and jumped onto the stool as the membranous bag bulged then popped, followed by more fluid flooding from the horse than Adam could have imagined she had the capacity to hold. "Jesus! What the fuck was that?"

"I think you tempted fate," Vance said with a wry smile. He patted Midnight's neck gently. "That's it girl. Now we're getting to the good stuff." Vance backed away from the horse and took his seat back on the stool. He glanced up at Adam still standing on his.

"What are you doing? Get down, we can't do anything now. It's all up to her."

"What did you think was wrong?" Adam asked, sitting down.

"I thought I saw placenta before the bag, but it must have just been where the bag was getting ready to go." Vance yawned widely. "Not that that'll stop Gregson from charging me an extra call out fee."

"Gregson?"

"The vet."

"Ah," Adam said with an understanding nod. "You haven't called him by name before. Only "the vet"."

"Really?" Vance look surprised. "That's mighty civil for me. I usually call *her* the gold-digging Witch of the West."

Adam was prevented from answering by Midnight easing onto the hay, lying on her side. Vance had said that the second stage of labor could last anything between five and fifteen minutes. But if she hadn't managed to get the foal out herself within thirty, they'd have to step in and help. Vance had laughed at the comical horror on Adam's face at the thought of actually having to get down and dirty. Adam settled down, a kaleidoscope of excited butterflies taking flight in the pit of his stomach. He'd never seen the miracle of life happening in all its gloriously gory detail before, and he felt like a little kid on Christmas morning. Okay… so he desperately hoped Midnight was going to push that foal out *tout suite*, but at the same time, he was more than ready to dive in if he had to.

He glanced at Vance beside him, seeing the same childish excitement that must surely be on his own face. Yet beneath it there was an underlying concern for his girl. Over the last couple of days, he'd glimpsed the Vance he knew hid behind the bravado, but now… right now… this was Vance at his most open. Heart on his sleeve for all to see. Adam smiled softly to himself. He liked it.

"Thanks for staying."

Adam shrugged as nonchalantly as he could, not taking his gaze off Midnight, who was beginning to huff and puff like a steam train. "No problem." He grinned at the nudge of Vance's knee against his own. Midnight began to whinny, and Adam could see her big stomach muscles tightening with the effort of forcing the foal down the birth canal. "Jesus," he hissed. "Is she okay?"

"She's doing good," Vance looked at his watch. "All we can do is wait."

"Shouldn't we do something?" Adam began to feel itchy inside his own skin, unable to keep still. "She's in pain, man."

Vance patted his knee. "That's because she's trying to crap out a horse, dude." He chuckled softly. "It's a good job you're gay. You'd be a nightmare in the delivery room."

"Shut up." Adam couldn't stop his leg from bouncing nervously. This whole miracle of life shit wasn't all it was cracked up to be. Midnight's soulful brown eyes kept rolling in her head as she pushed. All her energy concentrated on getting that baby out. He scrubbed a hand over his face. If he could have taken away her pain, he would have. He'd never felt so useless in his entire life.

"You'd better have a good reason for dragging me away from my date, Wolf."

Adam blinked and his mouth drop opened when the owner of that voice stepped into the stall. The woman was absolutely beautiful, with skin the color of ebony and eyes like limpid pools of dark chocolate. Yes, he was gay, but he knew beauty when he saw it, and damn, she was gorgeous. Not exactly what he'd expected the vet to look like. Neither was her ensemble. She wore a royal blue, skin-tight dress with spaghetti straps that couldn't have been any shorter if it had tried, along with the highest suede heels he'd ever seen.

"A date, Gregson?" Vance barked out a laugh. "You been sending out your flyin' monkeys to pick up guys again?"

"Jealousy is a terrible thing, Wolf." She walked across the stall and squatted behind the trembling horse. Her whole frosty demeanor immediately melted, her voice gentle. "How's it going, Momma?" Adam watched in stunned amazement as she stroked the horse's sweating neck, seemingly uncaring of the expensive dress she wore as she wiped her hand down the front of it. "I know it hurts, sweetie. We're gonna get this one out safe and sound. I promise." She shrugged off her shawl wrap and opened the bag she'd brought in with her. While she pulled on the long latex gloves she removed from the bag, she seemed to notice Adam for the first time and she grinned, clearly intrigued. "Well, hello there."

Her gaze slid slowly over Adam, lingering on his lips and then... other parts... that made him increasingly uncomfortable. "Hey, I'm—"

"Not for you," Vance said pointedly.

"Ignore him," Gregson countered. "You're...?"

"Adam Prentiss." Adam held out his hand and she shook it.

"Marla Gregson. Where have you been all my life?"

"Gregson." Vance's warning was clear.

She sighed dramatically and shook her head, "Typical. The prettiest ones are always gay. One of life's great ironies." She raised a hopeful eyebrow at Adam. "Any chance you swing both ways?"

"*Gregson.*"

Adam laughed. He liked her. "No, I'm sorry. As much as I have the utmost respect for your gender. You've got cooties and…," he shuddered dramatically, "girl parts."

"If you two have finished," Vance drawled sarcastically. "I think we're having a baby here."

Adam gasped. Two hooves were protruding from Midnight's 'girl parts'. "Holy cow."

Marla frowned. "Vance, how long since the bag ruptured?"

Vance checked his watch again. "Eleven minutes."

"There's a lot of blood." She looked up at him. "Did you see any placenta before the bag went?"

"I thought I saw a glimpse but then when I checked again, it was gone."

"Okay," she said firmly. "I want this foal out now. I can't see what's going on while he's still in there. Let's give her a hand."

Adam's gut tightened, but he remained on the stool, not wanting to get in the way. Vance's expression darkened, but other than that, he showed no emotion as he sprang into action. All Adam could do was sit back and watch.

Vance squatted beside Marla and pulled on the

gloves she handed him. "Right, when she strains, we need to ease him out. Don't pull, we're giving her a hand, not taking over."

"I know how to help a foaling," Vance snapped.

Marla ignored him and turned her full attention to Midnight. "Come on, old girl, nice big push."

Adam was surprised at the speed with which the foal was born once Vance and Marla helped ease it out. When its head entered the world, Marla cleared its nose and mouth of the amniotic sac. With a final push, the foal flopped onto the hay, its ribcage heaving as it took its first breaths outside of the womb. The birth itself had taken no more than a few minutes, but the amount of blood that followed had fear replacing Adam's amazed wonderment.

If he'd felt helpless before, it was magnified tenfold as he watched Marla and Vance struggle to stem the bleeding. From the clipped instructions being tossed back and forth, he managed to grasp that Midnight had internal bleeding and Marla was desperately trying to locate it. He'd never seen so much blood before. The hay surrounding the horse was stained dark red and getting darker. He wasn't a religious man, but he hoped, if there was a man upstairs, he would hear his silent plea. *Please don't let him lose her.*

Ten arduous minutes later, Marla sat back on her heels and ripped off her gloves, tossing them to the floor. She lifted a hand and Adam felt the tender compassion in her touch as she brushed her fingers through Vance's hair. "I'm sorry, Wolf."

Adam's breath hitched in his throat at the bob of Vance's Adam's apple as he obviously tried to keep his emotions in check. When the cowboy raised his head and Adam could see his eyes, the pain in them was unbearable. He was overwhelmed with the need to wrap the man up in his arms, but he wouldn't—not yet. All he could do was sit and watch.

Vance ripped off his own gloves and wiped his hands down the front of his already blood-stained jeans. Then he stood and approached the foal, who none of them had noticed getting to his feet and swaying on wobbly legs during the fight to save his mother. Vance picked up a handful of hay and began to rub down the foal with it, ridding him of what remained of the protective sac he'd spent almost a year inside. "Look at you," Vance murmured, his voice low and gentle. He glanced over his shoulder at Midnight and smiled, although Adam could see the sheen of tears in his eyes. "He's beautiful, Momma. You did a good job, but you rest now. I'll take it from here."

The lump in Adam's throat was so big, he was sure it was his heart, but he swallowed past it and got to his feet. He hunkered down beside Vance and the foal and picked up a handful of hay as he'd seen Vance do. Adam wiped the hay over the foal's coat without a word. He couldn't think of anything to say anyway, and the usual platitudes would be just that—platitudes. When Vance suddenly gripped his fingers and squeezed them firmly, Adam met his gaze and saw the appreciation in Vance's deep green eyes, words didn't seem that important.

*

Adam stood beneath the spray of the shower, eyes closed as the hot water cascaded over his skin, steam filling the tiny bathroom in the bunkhouse. The last couple of hours had seemed to pass in a blur. Marla and he had headed back to the main house, leaving Vance alone to say his goodbyes. After they'd broken the news to Walt, he and Travis had disappeared to deal with Midnight's body. While the boys dealt with the aftermath of death, Audrey dealt with the new life. She made some phone calls and sent Cody over to the Cartwright's for some milk pellets to tide them over until one of them could get to the feed store in the morning.

Marla had sat with Adam and Audrey at the kitchen table, his colleagues having already retired for the night. Adam had felt guilty laughing at some of the stories Marla told them, but he appreciated she was trying to lighten the mood. And some of the anecdotes she had about Vance over the years had his ribs aching and tears rolling down his face. Although Vance had made it seem there was animosity between them, the truth of the matter was very different. Adam found out they'd been best friends since junior high and they'd even gone to their senior prom together. Marla told him Vance came out shortly after that, and she was convinced she was responsible, citing she'd obviously been 'too much woman' for him.

After she'd left it had been almost one, and Vance had still not returned from the barn. Audrey had patted his hand gently and sent him off to bed, stating that Vance could be a while yet, so there was no sense in him waiting up. Adam had reluctantly acquiesced. Which was why he now stood beneath the shower, rinsing his body free of soap suds left behind by the shower gel he'd used. He turned off the shower and stepped out of the cubicle to grab a towel. The first he wrapped around his waist and secured it, before rubbing another over his hair. He gathered his wash bag and padded down the corridor in his bare feet to his room. There was a chill in the air, so he quickly dried himself off and pulled on sweatpants and a T-shirt.

Adam slipped beneath the covers and crossed his arms under his head. Staring up at the ceiling, he tried to erase the image of Vance, his fingers gently stroking the length of Midnight's neck as Adam had left the stall with Marla. He had held himself together, but Adam didn't need to be a genius to know Vance was on the verge of losing his steely control. Not that he would have ever let them see it. He sighed heavily and closed his eyes. There was no telling what time they'd be starting out in the morning, so there was nothing left to do but sleep—if he could.

Thirty minutes of tossing and turning later, he decided he couldn't. Couldn't sleep, couldn't settle, couldn't stop thinking about Vance.

Fuck it! Adam threw off the covers and clambered out of bed. *What am I doing?* He had no idea. Vance's face swam before his eyes, his green gaze filled with pain and he couldn't fight the need to see if he was okay. There was no way he was going to get a wink of sleep otherwise. All he had to do was walk into the main house and knock on Vance's door. Once he'd seen for himself that all was as it should be, he'd go back to bed. Easy—right? He refused to even listen to his inner voice, quickly slamming the door in his in its face before it opened its mouth.

The air was still sticky even at this hour, so Adam shoved his feet into his battered sneakers and sneaked out of the bunkhouse. He crossed the six feet of dirty to the house and opened the door, closing it gently behind him. Although it was dark, the moonlight cast shadows through the windows, and he knew his way to Vance's room, having woken him the day before. He stared at the door handle for a few minutes. What the hell was he doing? He didn't even know if Vance was in there for God's sake. Adam sighed and turned away, his intention to return to his room and get some sleep. Instead of acting like the heroine from one of Oprah's Book of the Month tomes. Then he heard footsteps from behind the door. *Balls.* Before he could come up with any more excuses as to why he was standing outside Vance's door in his pj's, Adam turned the handle and slipped inside the room.

Vance stood by the dresser, staring at Adam's reflection in the mirror above it. His damp hair had been combed back from his forehead, and a towel was secured around his waist. The cotton clung to his ass like a second skin and droplets of water traversed the muscles that rippled beneath his tanned flesh.

God, he's beautiful.

Adam met his gaze in the mirror and took a deep breath. "I just wanted to make sure you were okay." Vance acknowledged his concern with the hint of a smile. Adam swallowed. "So… are you? Okay?"

Vance turned to face him. He looked tired. As if the evening's events were etched into his skin. "Sure," he said, nonchalantly, but Adam wasn't fooled for a minute. "Horses die all the time out here. You get used to it."

"Stop being the big macho cowboy." Adam could hear the annoyance in his voice and tried to push it back. He hadn't come here to fight. "We both know she wasn't just a horse. You saved her. You gave her a second chance at the life she should have had. You gave her a real home. So, stop being so goddamn stoic. Not with me."

Vance crossed his arms over his chest and leaned against the dresser, staring Adam down. "Not with you? Why not with you? Are you suddenly somethin' special?"

Adam threw his hands up in the air and shook his head. "Fine," he said, his fingers curling around the door handle behind him. "Whatever. Wallow by yourself. I shouldn't have come."

Before he could turn the handle, Vance was at his back, pressed tight against him, his lips at Adam's ear. "Why did you come?" Adam gasped as Vance ground his hips into his ass. "Did you want to pick up where we left off?" His lips left a trail of fire on the sensitive skin of Adam's throat. "You came here for one thing, and we both know it."

Adam spun around and shoved Vance away from him. "I came because I wanted to know you were okay. I came because I thought you might want to talk. I came because you were in pain. I came because I thought you might need a friend. But you can't drop the guard, can you? Even after what we both witnessed tonight, what I shared with you today in my room, you still won't let me in." His frustration drove him on. "The great Vance Wolf don't need nobody. I get it. Well, fuck you."

"Adam, wait." Vance grabbed Adam's forearm before he could make good his escape. "Please… don't go." Adam looked into his eyes and saw anger. Anger at the situation. Anger at the world. But beneath it all, sorrow and regret. Vance Wolf stripped bare. "I'm sorry. I just don't… I don't know how to—"

Adam closed the gap between them and cupped Vance's face in his hands. "Ssh, it's okay. It's okay." Staring into Vance's eyes he knew, without a doubt, his father could go fuck himself. *He* wanted this man— *him.*

They seemed to move at the same time. Their mouths came together in mutual need. This time Adam wasn't giving away control. *He* was driving this bus, and Vance could just buckle up and hold on tight.

Adam slid his hands over Vance's shoulders, his chest and around the small of his back. Vance's skin was smooth and soft under his touch and he couldn't wait to follow the same path with his lips. He walked Vance backward until the back of his legs hit the edge of the bed and he broke the kiss, his fingers at the towel around Vance's waist. They both panted heavily, breathing in each other's exhalations, gazes locked as Adam pulled on the thin cotton square separating them—yes he had clothes on, but they didn't count right now and weren't going to be on for long—and then let it drop to the floor. He took a step back and let his gaze take in the curves, the planes and the ridges of muscle and sinew, lingering on Vance's already semi-hard shaft where it jutted from a closely trimmed bed of dark curls.

"You like what you see?" Vance's voice was rich and smooth, like aged whiskey tumbling over ice.

"You're beautiful," Adam whispered in returned. "Absolutely fuckin' beautiful." He meant it. Vance looked as though he could have been carved out of marble by Michelangelo himself—and he wasn't talking about the horse he'd been riding. "Lie down."

For once, Vance didn't argue and did as he was told. Adam watched through lowered lashes while the cowboy eased himself into the center of the king-size bed and settled onto the pillows. His tanned flesh stood in stark relief against the crisp white sheets. Adam's breath caught in his throat as Vance smiled languidly and moistened his lips with the tip of his tongue. He grabbed the hem of his T-shirt, yanked it over his head and sent it to join the towel on the floor. Then he tucked his thumbs into the waistband of his sweatpants and eased them down his legs, kicking them off and leaving himself open to Vance's gaze. As he had scrutinized every inch of Vance's flesh, he stood for a moment while Vance did the same. He was unable not to revel in the surge of heat flooding through him as Vance's green eyes darkened further.

Adam smiled softly as he crawled up the bed on all fours. "You like what *you* see, cowboy?"

"I have since you arrived, and you know it." Vance's fingers curled around the back of Adam's neck and pulled him down to bring their lips back together.

Adam grabbed Vance's wrists and forced his hands against the pillows, holding him down. He ravaged Vance's mouth, coaxing his tongue into an ageless dance, tasting toothpaste and beer. Vance must have foregone the coffee in favor of a Bud, not that he blamed him, and not that he cared, it was intoxicating. He couldn't get enough of Vance's lips on his, the heat of miles of sun-bronzed flesh against his own. He wanted more. He wanted it all.

Vance moaned in complaint when Adam broke the kiss, then gasped as he slid his lips the length of Vance's throat. Adam smiled, reveling in the sounds his touch drew from him. He placed wet, open-mouthed kisses to every inch of heated skin and circled Vance's nipples with the tip of his tongue.

"*Adam.*"

His name on Vance's lips sent sparks throughout his body, and his cock throbbed with delicious anticipation. He moaned low in his throat, pulling Vance's flesh between his lips. "Say it again." He nipped at the jut of Vance's hipbone.

"*Adam.* Jesus… *Adam.*"

Adam pressed his face to the hair surrounding Vance's cock and inhaled deeply. The muskiness of Vance's natural scent combined with the shower gel he'd used filled Adam's senses. The soft velvety skin of Vance's shaft brushed his cheek and he raised himself on his hands, his gaze predatory as it captured and held Vance's. The cowboy's expletive was abruptly cut off as Adam licked a stripe the length of his shaft and slid his lips over the crown, sucking him into his mouth. Vance threw his head back onto the pillow and a stream of whispered litany fell from his lips as Adam worked his cock. Adam felt Vance's fingers grip the short strands of his hair and moaned around the engorged flesh in his mouth. The taste of him was nectar. It lit up his tongue, heightened his senses and left him wanting more. He cupped Vance's heavy sac, rolling the swollen balls in his palm. The head of Vance's cock hit the back of this throat and he swallowed around it, feeling the involuntary thrust of Vance's hips into his mouth.

"Yes… fuck… Adam," Vance whimpered, "gonna cum."

Adam curled his fingers around the base of Vance's

cock and lifted his head, letting it fall from his lips with an obscenely wet sound. "Uh-uh, not yet," he said with a wicked smile. "I want you to lose it inside me. I'm gonna ride you, cowboy." He moved up Vance's body and kissed him, hard, fast and dirty. "New York style." Adam straddled Vance's thighs, and his breath caught in his throat as Vance's hand closed around both Adam's and his own cock, and he jacked them together. *"Fuck!"* His heart beat frantically in his chest and he curled his fingers into Vance's thighs. "Lube? Condom?"

Vance threw his arm out and yanked open the top drawer of the nightstand, then scrabbled inside. With a practiced ease Adam didn't want to think about right now, Vance pulled out a bottle of lube and a foil packet and slapped them into Adam's outstretched palm.

With some practiced ease of his own, he ripped open the condom and rolled it down Vance's cock, then lubed his length before he rubbed more of the water-based gel around his hole. He positioned himself and then reached behind him to take Vance's cock in his hand and press it to his opening.

"Wait!" Vance gasped. "What about you? I don't wanna hurt you."

Adam shook his head and began to ease down onto Vance. "Just shut up and keep still." He closed his eyes as Vance slid inside, stretching him wide. Breath falling from his lips in short, sharp gasps, Adam kept going until he was fully seated in Vance's lap. He took a few moments to catch his breath and to savor the utter completeness he felt at being surrounded by the man beneath him. He opened his eyes and smiled down at Vance, who stared at him, transfixed, lips parted, his chest heaving. Then Adam began to move. Slowly at first. Lifting himself up and down Vance's cock, Vance's hands gripping his hips. Awkward at first until they found a rhythm, Adam picked up the pace until he was bouncing on Vance's cock like Tigger on speed. Each thrust drove Vance deeper, and if he just adjusted his angle a little—*fuck*—the thick mushroom-ridged head of Vance's cock nailed his prostate over and over.

Adam was lifted on a wave of ecstasy, no longer in control of his own body as it sought release. He'd never felt as connected to another person as he did right now. Sex had always been a means to an end. Getting off. But this, right here, with this man, he finally understood what all those country songs and Bridget Jones had been talking about.

His name was a mantra on Vance's lips and the sound of it and the slap of skin against skin, pushed Adam closer to the edge. He thrust up into Vance's fingers as they jacked him rough and fast, and back down onto Vance's cock, chasing his release. Flying high and higher, his orgasm approaching at warp speed, Vance met his downward thrust with a guttural cry and Adam felt him throb inside him as he came. That was all Adam needed. He shot streams of white onto Vance's chest. His body lost all rhythm and he threw his head back to stare sightlessly at the ceiling as waves of sensation flowed through him.

Chapter seven

Adam collapsed onto the mattress beside him and Vance desperately tried to remember how to breathe. His chest heaved and his lungs burned. If that was how they did it in New York, he didn't care if he ever went to another rodeo. He shoved his fingers into his hair, needing to hold onto something, sure he was going to shatter into a million pieces from the intensity of the orgasm he'd experienced. His brain obviously didn't have enough blood left in it to form proper sentences, because only one word bounced around his skull—*fuck!*

Being inside Adam had felt like coming home. That was the only way he could describe it. The closeness. The intensity. He'd never felt that with anyone. *Anyone.* He scrubbed his hands over his face and turned his head to gaze at Adam's face on the pillow beside him. Adam's eyes were closed tight, and Vance frowned in sudden concern. He hadn't let Vance take the time to prepare him. *Shit!* He rolled onto his side, unmindful of the rapidly drying semen on his chest. "Adam?" he shook his shoulder. "Adam? Baby, are you okay?"

"Baby?" Adam opened his left eye and looked at him, his lips twitching. "Did I just hear big, bad Vance Wolf say…*baby?*"

"Shut up," Vance flopped onto his back. "Remind

me not to bother checking if you're still alive next time." Adam rolled over on top of him, forcing a rush of air from his lungs. He obviously didn't care about cum either.

"Who says there's going to be a next time?" Adam said, a solemn expression on his face. "This is a one night only deal, cowboy."

Vance huffed out a laugh. "That would have been a whole lot more convincing without the semi pressed against my leg."

"Well I didn't say it was a one *time* thing," Adam teased, "just a one *night* thing."

Vance shook his head and yawned widely. "You're funny. You ever thought about stand-up?" The night's events were catching up with him. Not forgetting he'd just been 'hi-ho silvered' to within an inch of his life. "Good thing we didn't do this three days ago."

"Why's that?"

"'Cause I'd never have let you out of this bed," Vance said softly, capturing Adam's lips in a tender kiss. "And it would have been a cryin' shame to miss those creases." He grimaced at the stickiness between them. Rolling away from Adam he pushed himself up and then climbed out of bed, tossing instructions over his shoulder for Adam to stay exactly where he was, before quickly crossing the room to the en suite. After stripping off the condom, he wrapped it in some tissue and dropped it into the waste bin—making a mental note to empty the damn thing himself. He then grabbed a washcloth and wet it under a stream of warm water, rung out the excess and rubbed at his stomach with it. Finally, he dried off with a fresh towel.

Vance rinsed the washcloth and wrung it out again,

turning off the light as he passed it on his way back into the bedroom, cloth in hand and towel slung over his shoulder. He smiled down at Adam, stretched languidly against the pillows, his pale grey eyes darkened to almost black. Vance didn't think he'd ever seen him look more wanton. He tilted his head as he moved the navy washcloth across the pale honey-colored skin of Adam's belly and around his cock. Well, maybe he had. When he'd gazed up at Adam as he'd ridden him with an intensity and purpose Vance had never felt before. Adam had been the perfect picture of desire, need and wanton passion—and he'd never looked more beautiful. He dried Adam's now damp skin and then tossed the items to the floor; eternally grateful he'd cleaned and put away the toy that had lain there before them.

"Get your ass in here, cowboy," Adam grumbled, although his smile belied his annoyance. "I'm gettin' cold."

"You're gettin' mighty used to orderin' me around, City-Boy." Vance slid back onto the mattress beside Adam and pulled the covers over them. He settled against the pillows and shivered when Adam wriggled beneath his arm and curled around him. But it wasn't from cold. Vance swallowed hard and then wished he hadn't, because he felt Adam chuckle vibrate against his shoulder before he spoke.

"What?"

"Nothin'." Vance should have known better than to hope Adam would be fobbed off, when Adam's only response was an inelegant snort. He'd do more than snort if he knew the jumbled thoughts bouncing around his head like a pinball. He'd laugh his ass off. Some big macho cowboy he was.

"The whirring of the cogs in your brain is keeping me awake." Adam said pointedly a few moments later. "Do you want me to go?"

"No!" Vance pulled Adam even closer to him. "No. Just not used to it."

Adam rose onto his elbow and grabbed Vance's chin, forcing him to meet his gaze. "What are you trying to say?" He kissed Vance's lips gently. "If you're worried I'll find out you're not the tough Texan rancher you purport to be, don't. I've looked into your eyes and seen your heart, cowboy. I *know* who you are."

"You do, huh?" Vance smiled and took the fingers cupping his chin in his own and pressed his lips to them. He didn't doubt it for a moment. He had no idea why, or even how, but Adam knew him. In fact, there had never been a man who'd even come close to getting under his skin. So why him? "I'm not used to that either," he said, studying Adam's face. "Someone in my bed... in my head." He stroked his knuckles along Adam's jaw. "Who are you, City-Boy?"

"I'm the Lone Ranger to your Tonto," Adam replied, kissing him again. "The Rawhide to your Bonanza. The Curly to your Mo. The—"

Vance put his hand over Adam's mouth, stopping the words in their tracks. "If you say the frank to my beans, I swear to God I'm gonna..."

Adam chuckled behind his hand and then batted it away, his expression solemn for real this time. "Is that true?" he asked. "You've not had anyone in your bed before?"

Vance shrugged. "Never met anyone I wanted to spend the night with." It was true. Heated hook-ups were much more his style. Not something he was necessarily proud of. But it had suited him and them—until now.

"Just when I think you can't possibly surprise me; you go and do it again." Adam smiled and kissed him. "I'm sorry about Midnight. I know how much she meant to you."

Vance nodded; his heart warmed by the compassion in Adam's eyes. "She was so stubborn, you know? She shouldn't have even carried that foal to term, but she was determined he was gonna make it. She did what all good mommas do, she made sure her baby was safe before she left."

"You're a good man, Vance Wolf," Adam said softly. "She was lucky she found you. And so am I."

Swiftly rolling them both over so Adam was beneath him, Vance kissed him, swiping his tongue over Adam's full lower lip before he pulled back. "I guess that makes three of us."

*

If falling asleep in Adam's arms had been weird, waking up in them was even more so. At first Vance couldn't figure out why he was so hot, until he'd opened his eyes and found that, at some point during the night, Adam had decided to make him the little spoon. He attempted to move but Adam's arm tightened around his waist and he huffed a sigh into the nape of his neck. Vance smiled to himself and swallowed down a chuckle. *Goddamn, Vance Wolf likes being the little spoon.* If anyone had said that to him a week ago, he'd have walked away and left them... lyin' there. *I guess you really do learn something new every day.* Adam Prentiss was definitely an experience he could get more than used to, that was for dang sure.

"You're thinking again. I can smell burning."

"Wow, five am and still funny," Vance replied. "There's hope for you yet, Prentiss."

"Can't we play hooky today?" Adam nuzzled the back of his neck and Vance closed his eyes, giving himself over to the sensations caused by the rough scrape of Adam's stubble against his skin.

"I'd say that's the best idea you've had all week," Vance said, wriggling his ass against Adam's morning wood. "But we've got calves to rope, business to tease and a cookout to prepare for. Momma thought it would be nice to invite some of the neighbors. Show you guys a real slice of Texas life." He turned in Adam's arms, so they were face to face. "Although right now, I think we have more pressing things to think about." He wriggled his hips again, catching Adam's gasp between his lips as he kissed him. Of course, the man would taste good, even first thing in the morning. Adam moaned low in his throat and the sound of it sent sparks of heat to Vance's hardening shaft.

Vance's breath fell in short sharp gasps as their mouths parted and came back together time and again, unable to get enough of each other. He was being swept away on a sea of sensation, waves lifting him up and crashing him back onto the sand, Adam's hands everywhere, touching, caressing, strok—

"Vance, c'mon. We've got work to do. Oh, my Lord!"

Vance all but threw Adam out of bed at the sound of his mother's voice from where she stood in the now open doorway. "*Mom!*" He bit back the curse on the tip of his tongue. "Did you forget how to knock?"

"Did you forget how to lock?" She snapped back.

Then her expression softened. "Mornin', Adam honey. Coffee's on, let's go, lots to do today."

"Um… mornin, Mz Audrey."

"Well don't just lie there," Audrey admonished, waving a hand at them. "Once you've finished your business, I'll see you in the kitchen."

"*Momma!*"

"Please," Audrey shook her head, her expression derisive. "How do you think *you* got here?"

"Not like *this*!"

"Such a prude," she mumbled before she dropped Adam a wink and then closed the door behind her.

"I'm sorry," Vance said on a sigh. "Any chance you had of staying in the closet this week just vanished quicker 'an a smoke signal in a hurricane. She's probably in the kitchen making the 'Vance hearts Adam' banner right now."

"Aww," Adam rolled over on top of him and fluttered his eyelashes. "Do you?"

"Do I what?"

"Heart me."

"Shut up," Vance pushed Adam back onto the mattress and attempted to get out of bed. His progress was stilled by Adam's arm around his waist.

"Where are you going? We've got business to finish. Your momma said."

Vance snorted inelegantly and extricated himself from Adam's grip. He turned to gaze down at him and shook his head. "There is so much wrong with that statement I don't even know where to start." He threw a pillow at Adam and laughed when it hit him square in the face. "Now get up, you've gotta sneak back to your room. I'll be thinkin' of you in that freezing cold bathroom in the bunkhouse while I take a long… hot… naked shower right here in my own personal piece of tiled heaven."

He had to concede that maybe that was one tease too far, and he might have deserved it when Adam leaped out of bed, pushed him back onto the mattress and sprinted into the en suite, then slammed the door behind him and shot the lock home. Vance flopped back onto the mattress and stared up at the ceiling, a big grin on his face. Yeah, he definitely deserved that.

He heard the shower turn on and his grin widened as he imagined Adam stepping under the spray. He had no idea what had brought Adam to Wolf Creek, be it fate, destiny… God, and right now, in that moment, he didn't care. All that mattered was that Adam was here—and Vance had no intention of ever letting him go.

*

Vance sipped at his beer. The ice cold liquid slid over his taste buds and down his throat and his tongue chased the droplets of moisture on his lips. The cookout was drawing to a close, and the sun was slowly sinking below the horizon. As usual, his mother had outdone herself. It seemed as though everyone they knew had attended. The Cartwrights, the Gillespies, and the Walters along with the passel of children and grandchildren playing rough and tumble on the grass. Together with most of the town, with the sheriff being the only noticeable absentee. Not that that had been much of a surprise. He shook his head fondly as Jacob, the Cartwrights' youngest grandson, zoomed by his chair, followed by his father in hot pursuit. The kids had been ushered away from his mother's flowerbeds more than once, and he had the feeling Jacob was coming perilously close to a visit to the woodshed.

"You're lookin' pleased with yourself," Marla said, sitting on the lawn chair beside him. "Would I be wrong in thinkin' it's got somethin' to do with that gorgeous suit I met the other night?"

"Shut up," Vance said, making a failed attempt to keep the smile from his voice. "When I want your opinion, I'll ask for it. Which will probably be around about the twelfth of never."

"Ooh," Marla crowed excitedly. "So, we like this one." She nudged him with her shoulder. "Does he feel the same?"

Vance nudged back. "I think so."

"Well, Momma already likes him, so that's a reason to hog-tie him and lock him in the fruit cellar, right there."

"You are too twisted for color TV, Claree," Vance huffed, shaking his head at her.

"Whoa, if you're quoting Steel Magnolias at me, it must be serious."

"Shut up." Vance gazed around the crowd and found Adam and Graham laughing at something his momma was saying. By the way they kept glancing over, it didn't take a genius to figure out it concerned him. "Dear God, can't that woman keep anythin' secret?"

Marla chuckled softly. "What do you reckon it is?" she asked. "The time you got your head stuck in the spindles of the school stairs, and they had to grease you up to get you out?" Vance groaned. "Or the time when she caught you with Scotty Lambert in the hayloft when you were seven, measuring your winkies?"

"Jesus," Vance hissed, turning to look at her. "You think she'd go that far?"

"Let's hope it's not the time she caught you in the hayloft with Eddie Mitchell doing somethin' else with your winkies."

"I hate you."

"I know."

As the men talked animatedly with his mother, trying to balance their beers and plates of food at the same time, Vance let his mind wander to the morning's activities.

Adam may have locked him out of the bathroom, but it hadn't been for long. Vance had been chuckling to himself when he'd heard the lock being pulled back and the door open. He'd stood up and padded across the room, the sight of Adam leaning against the tiles in the shower cubicle, slowly jacking his cock, had him choking on his own breath. Heated kisses, mutual blow-jobs and then the sensual reciprocal washing of their bodies followed, and Vance had to agree with Adam that it had been a very satisfying way to the start the day.

Luckily, Adam's secret remained safe to fight another day because he didn't bump into any of his colleagues as he made good his escape from Vance's room. Although if he'd blushed any more at breakfast Vance was more than certain they'd figure out something was going on with him. Of course, it probably hadn't helped that Vance kept playing footsie with him and took an obscene amount of time to eat a banana—in a possibly obscene way. He'd known it was mean, but damn if he didn't like to make that boy blush.

After they'd set up the tables and chairs and pulled

the grill out of the barn for the cookout later, Vance knew from experience that getting in his mother's way was *not* a good idea. He'd told Cory and Travis to saddle the horses and they'd ridden out to the south paddock to do a little roping to keep them out of trouble. He'd sat atop Goliath, watching the other men on their respective steeds, trotting and then cantering across the green fields, cutting a swathe through the herd. He'd laughed when Phil whooped loudly and waved his hat in the air, trying to urge Raphael into a gallop. Phil had obviously been having such a great time, he hadn't had the heart to tell him Raphael only had two gears—walk and wait a while.

Vance took another draw from the bottle he held in his hand and swallowed it down. When his mother had suggested this whole cowboy camp thing, to say he'd been skeptical would have been an understatement. But he had to admit. They were a good group and he'd had a lot more fun than he'd ever expected. And that wasn't because he'd found Adam, although that had been a definite bonus. Maybe it hadn't been such a bad idea after all.

His bottle paused on its way to his mouth as he caught Adam's gaze, and he narrowed his eyes against the glare of the sun. Adam's grey eyes held intent, heat and *right-the-fuck-now*. Even with the few feet separating them, Vance could see exactly what he was thinking, and he snaked out his tongue to moisten suddenly dry lips. He felt a surge of satisfaction as Adam's lips parted in response. Vance watched Adam excuse himself to Audrey and Graham, then turn deliberately on his heel and walk toward the barn.

"Yep," Marla said beside him. "Must've been the

Eddie Mitchell story."

"Shut up," Vance replied, handing her his beer. He got up and meandered across the lawn, stopping to pass a few words with some of the neighbors, before following the same path Adam had taken minutes before. If he could hear Marla chuckling or feel his mother's stare on his back, he didn't care. He was firmly fixed on one person, and it wasn't either of them.

Inside the barn, the coming dusk cast shadows and dappled light through hayloft window. Vance strode purposefully toward the center of the barn and the ladder that was the only route to the hayloft. He smiled when he saw the bandana Adam had tied to one of the rungs, leaving him in no doubt where his City-Boy waited.

Vance climbed the ladder and stepped into the loft, his gaze searching for Adam in the semi-dark. His breath caught in his throat at the sight of Adam sitting on one bale of hay and leaning against another, his jeans open and his hand inside his boxers, languidly stroking himself. He looked the picture of wanton desire, his Stetson pulled low over his forehead, staring at Vance from beneath lowered lashes, his thighs spread wide, lips parted in invitation. Not that Vance needed any. He was hard enough to cut rock already and was shaking so much he was unsure whether or not he'd make it to Adam on the newborn foal legs that had replaced his own. Vance groaned low in his throat when Adam took out his cock, hard and throbbing, pearls of pre-cum glinting on the head in the low light.

"Don't just stand there, cowboy," Adam said softly. "What're are you waiting for?"

Vance dropped to his knees and crawled across the

loft until he reached Adam, then slid his hands up the outside of Adam's legs and settled between his thighs. He gazed into Adam's eyes for a few moments and then dipped his head to take him into his mouth. The salty sweet taste burst over Vance's taste buds and he moaned around the shaft as he took him in to the root. The scent of male heat invaded his nostrils as he rubbed his nose against the trim curls surrounding Adam's cock and he lifted off quickly, gagging slightly and leaving a trail of saliva behind him.

"Fuck, Vance. You look so fuckin' good with me in your mouth."

"You taste so sweet, baby. I'll never get enough of you." Vance curled his fingers around the shaft and then took the head back between his lips. Then he set up a rhythm of simultaneous sucking and jerking as he brought Adam to the edge and back so many times, the man was a quivering mass of need beneath him.

Instinctively knowing Adam was close, Vance let go his cock and manhandled him swiftly so that Adam was on his knees in front of him, leaning on the bale of hay he had been sat upon, his ass beckoning him in. *Fuck! I haven't got anything!*

"In my back pocket," Adam grunted, glancing over his shoulder, sweat-damped hair sticking to his forehead.

Vance grinned widely as he rummaged around in Adam's jeans. "You planned this?"

"Might have thought about it." Adam panted, his breath hissing between his teeth. "C'mon, baby. I can't wait much longer."

With the brief thought that he may have just broken the land speed record for lubing up and rolling on a condom, Vance rubbed what was left of the lube from the small tube against Adam's hole. He pressed hungry, open-mouthed kisses to the side of Adam's neck and pushed a finger inside him, reveling in the animalistic grunts Adam couldn't contain. Pulling out, he gripped his cock and lined it up, then thrust as slowly as he could until he slipped past the tight ring of muscle and into the dark, wet heat beyond. It was like falling. Adam held onto him so tightly he got light-headed and it took all his willpower not to just pound into him until he had nothing left to give.

"Jesus," Vance hissed, biting his lip and holding still as he waited for Adam to give him the signal that he was ready. It was only a few moments before the muttered, "Do it," and the roll of Adam's hips gave him the indication he needed. Vance pulled out almost all the way and then slid back in, his thrust long and deep, searching for the rhythm that was comfortable for both of them.

He teased Adam with short sharp thrusts, interspersed with thrusts so deep and hard he couldn't tell where he ended, and Adam began. Shared open-mouthed awkward over the shoulder kisses that now seemed to be the perfect way to kiss. Held Adam with his arm around his waist so they were back to chest, Adam's hand curled around the back of his neck, holding them together. Every movement was more intense than the last and soon they'd been reduced to incoherent grunts and hissed 'yeses' into the cooling night air.

Adam came first, spilling onto the hay and Vance's hand as he stroked him to completion. Vance followed moments later when Adam clamped down on him like a vice and literally dragged his orgasm from him. An orgasm of such intensity he saw spots behind his closed lids, and it felt as though his cock would never stop pumping, his seed warming his flesh inside the condom as it left him.

When it was over, he reluctantly pulled out of Adam and collapsed onto his back on the hay, smiling happily when Adam tumbled down beside him. Vance chuckled softly to himself and thanked his lucky stars his mother hadn't walked into the barn today. When she'd caught him with Eddie Mitchell, they'd been giving each other a hand-job and her eyes had nearly popped out of her head. She might have fallen down the ladder if she'd seen how far his hayloft experience had come. *Come.* He chuckled again and turned his head to gaze at Adam beside him. If he was honest. He was beginning to think this whole cowboy camp thing may have been the single best idea his mother had ever had.

"Do you think anyone noticed we were gone?" Adam asked, quickly stuffing himself back into his pants and buttoning his jeans.

"I think you need some new blood in your department if they didn't. 'Cause they're obviously stupid." Vance dealt with the condom quickly and wrapped it in an old bit of tissue from his pocket, then slipped it into his jacket to dispose of when he got to his room. He raised himself onto his elbow and leaned in to kiss Adam soundly, tasting the remnants of the beer he'd been drinking.

"I could stay here forever," Adam mumbled, stroking Vance's bangs back from his forehead. He stared at him until Vance became uncomfortable under such scrutiny and began to fidget.

"What—?"

"What would you say if I said I didn't want to leave tomorrow?"

Vance gazed at Adam, open-mouthed and completely stunned. His stomach tightened nervously, and his mouth was suddenly dryer than the Sahara in a heat wave. He swallowed past the lump in his throat that felt a lot like his heart. *What* would *he say?* Would he go with his head, which had always told him the land was his life and he didn't need anything or anyone else. Or would he listen to his heart. The heart that beat out another's name for the first time in his life? What did he really have to offer Adam, way out here? Far away from the city life he'd known for so long. Could he make him happy enough to stay? Because if he didn't, would Vance be able to survive the fallout?

Adam paled and Vance swallowed, knowing he was taking his silence as rejection. "What would I say?" His voice sounded gruff with emotion and he really didn't care about retaining his masculinity, not right now. Adam nodded and Vance ran a shaking hand through his own hair. Was the risk worth it? He gazed down at Adam, so vulnerable, so hopeful, and a slow smile spread across Vance's lips. "I'd say you'd have to learn how to throw a rope."

"Seriously?"

Vance pulled Adam into his arms. "I must be plum crazy," he said softly, "but yes, seriously. I don't want you to leave tomorrow any more than you wanna go. Stay with me." Adam's response was to kiss him heatedly and Vance melted into his embrace. He had no idea what was happening between them, but he knew deep down it was worth taking a chance on. If he didn't, he'd regret it for the rest of his life. "But what about your job?" Vance asked, when Adam finally let him up for air.

Adam shook his head. "Don't you worry about that. I'll take care of it."

"Don't you have to give notice, or somethin'? You can't just walk out, can you?" Vance frowned as Adam gazed off into the middle distance, retreating inside himself for a moment.

"I'll take care of it," Adam said, his smile returning to his face. "Nothin' else matters. Just you and me."

"You do realize you've started droppin' your 'g's', don't you, City-Boy?" Vance kissed him again. "Maybe the country *has* gotten under your skin."

"I think you might be right, cowboy." Adam stood up and held out his hand to Vance, hauling him to his feet. "I think you might be right." He raised his arms over his head and stretched, his T-shirt riding up and revealing a strip of pale skin above his waistband. Although Vance kind of got the idea that was the intent, judging by the glint in his eye. "Come on, before we *are* missed. I can't wait to see the look on the guys' faces when I tell them I'm not going back. And there's a few other things I need to tell them, too."

Vance ushered Adam toward the ladder. "Babe, I don't think it's going to be as big a surprise as you think."

"What?" Adam paused on the fourth rung down and looked up at him. "You think they know?"

"We almost shook the loft off the barn. Trust me, Adam, *they* know."

They walked beside each other pass the horses in their stalls, their knuckles brushing as they did. Vance didn't think he'd ever been this happy—*ever*. Even walking next to Adam filled him with a contentment he'd never experienced. He gave an internal shake of his head. Was that even possible, or had he completely lost his mind? Perhaps one late night rerun of Oprah too many had tipped him over the edge? Maybe…. He blinked owlishly as they exited the barn. Everyone was gone.

The tables and chairs were empty, and everything had been cleared away. Adam's head whipped around as fast as Vance's did and they stared at each other. *How fuckin' long were we in there?* He could read his own thought as clear as day on Adam's face. Vance shrugged and scrubbed a hand through his hair. "Um… oops?"

"I think we've got some esplainin' to do," Adam said in a not unbelievable Spanish accent and Vance slung his arm around Adam's shoulders.

"C'mon then, Lucy, you can go in first." He bussed Adam's cheek as they walked up the porch steps to the open front door. "And don't forget about the second floorboard before the kitchen. It creaks."

"You're such a jerk," Adam giggled, but Vance noticed he still counted the floorboards as they approached the kitchen. "She's gonna ground me, isn't she?"

"She might." Vance grinned and squeezed Adam's shoulders, propelling him in front of him. "Just remember, if she uses your *full* name—run."

"Adam, Vance? That you?"

Audrey's voice floated toward them from the kitchen and Vance immediately felt like a naughty teenager. Not that that stopped him giggling like one.

Adam elbowed him in the side and stood up straight, clearing his throat before he dragged Vance into the room behind him.

"Hey, what's—?" Adam had stopped dead in front of him, and Vance barreled into him. He gazed around the assembled group at the kitchen table and frowned. What the hell was wrong with everybody? They all looked as though they'd seen a ghost. Then his gaze found the reason why. At the head of the table, where his father used to, and his mother should be seated was Andrew Blackwell. Vance's gut tightened. *What the fuck is he doing here?* "Momma?" he asked, but she didn't answer him.

"Vance," Blackwell said, that slimy shark's grin on his face. "How nice to see you again. Adam sounded as though he was having so much fun, I just had to come and see for myself."

Vance's gut tightened further. "Adam?" He glanced at the man beside him. The man he'd just given his everything to. "Adam?" Adam's gaze pleaded with him, but he only managed to say half of his name before Blackwell cut him off.

"Van—"

"Yes, *Adam*." Blackwell's tone was conversational, clearly enjoying every minute. But every minute of what? "My *son*."

Chapter eight

Adam gazed out of the window. Not that he could see anything but black. But he hadn't really expected anything else at thirty-six thousand feet.

"Can I get you another drink, sir?"

He smiled at the stewardess. "No, thank you." He handed her his empty glass. "I'm going to need my wits about me when we land."

"You have family in Austin?"

"I hope so." Adam turned away from her confused expression and returned to his gazing. She obviously took the hint, because he saw her walk away out of the corner of his eye, and he heaved a sigh of relief. He knew she was only being polite and doing her job, but he was not in the mood for niceties. It had been a very long two weeks and this was his only shot at making it right. If Vance would let him.

He closed his eyes and leaned back against the neck pillow the stewardess had handed him earlier. Two weeks without seeing or even speaking to Vance had felt like a lifetime. Not that he hadn't tried to talk to him. But it was a little difficult to hold a conversation with someone who either didn't answer the phone, or only picked it up long enough to hang up on you. He could hardly blame him.

The look on Vance's face would haunt him forever.

He'd never seen such pain clearly etched in every line. Well, until he'd caught sight of his own reflection in the car's side mirror as they drove away from the main house in his father's SUV. He'd seen every iota of Vance's pain in his own eyes and had nobody to blame for it but himself. The memory of that night and the last two weeks rushed toward him and he tried to back away, didn't want to re-live it. But he was given little choice and sighed as the crashing waves flooded his senses.

"Son? What are you talking about?" Vance's gaze flitted between Blackwell and Adam. "What the hell are you doing here, Blackwell?"

"I came to see my son." Adam wanted to run to his father and press his hand over his mouth. Anything to make him stop saying that word. "You see, Adam has been ignoring my calls for the last few days, so when the mountain won't come to Mohammed…"

"What are you talking about?" Vance asked, confusion all over his face. "Adam? What's he talking about? What is he talking *about?*"

Adam flinched as Vance's voice rose, his only response to open and close his mouth like a stranded bass. He couldn't form any words. How could his father do this? Why hadn't he realized his father *would* do this? He should have been prepared. If he'd only been prepared. His silence was all the answer Vance needed. Adam's heart ached in his chest as Vance's shoulders slumped. The fight leaving him in an instant as he realized the truth.

"You're his son?"

He found his voice. "Vance, please let me ex—"

"You're his *son*?"

"If you'll just let me ex—"

"Answer the fuckin' question you bastard! You're his *son*? You're *his* son? *You're* his son?"

Adam shook his head, but said softly, "Yes."

Vance sank into a chair and Adam moved toward him but was stopped in his tracks by a single word. "Don't."

"I was going to tell you." Adam began to babble. "I was going to tell you everything. Who I was, why he sent me here—" He snapped his lips shut when Vance turned his head to stare at him, his beautiful green eyes cold and distant.

"He *sent* you here?" Disbelief filled Vance's gaze. "This was a set up? The whole thing? You… and me?"

"Well, well, well, so you did take my advice and use any means necessary," Blackwell said, laughing cruelly. Adam turned on his heel and glared at the older man.

"Just shut the fuck up!"

"Dippin' your wick in some inferior stock must have given you some balls, Adam." Blackwell stood up and stared him down. "But don't push your luck, son. Your mother wouldn't like it."

Adam flinched at the undisguised threat in his father's tone and turned back to Vance. He reached out his hand and snatched it back when Vance all but growled at him in response. "Vance, please. I can explain everything. I wasn't going back, remember? I was going to tell him I was done, with all of it. Please, look at me. If you'd only let me—"

"Get out." Vance's warm rich voice was low and angry.

"Vance."

"Get. Out." Vance repeated the order and stood up, closing the gap between him and Adam, getting right up in Adam's face in an attempt to intimidate him. To give him his due it was working, but Adam had a whole lot more to lose than a punch in the face.

"No."

"Momma, hand me my gun."

"Vance!"

Vance turned his gaze to Blackwell and Adam swallowed at the total disconnection on his face. "If you don't get him off my land, I'll start shootin'." He looked back at Adam, a sneer curling his lip. "I won't ask twice."

"No," Adam whispered, tears pricking behind his eyes. *This couldn't be it—could it? It couldn't be over.*

"Mr Blackwell," Audrey said firmly, moving to stand beside Vance and taking his arm. "I think it would be wise if you do as my son says—now."

"Sir? Sir?"

Adam opened his eyes and tried to focus on the stewardess who loomed over him. "Yes?"

"Seatbelt sign's on, we're preparing to land." She nodded with a bright smile as he complied with her instructions and then moved on down the cabin.

Adam suppressed a yawn and quickly covered his mouth as it threatened to defeat him. He must have dozed off while he'd been lost in his thoughts. No matter. He thought of the paperwork in his backpack in the storage compartment above his head. Inside was the report he'd found in his father's safe at the office. It was amazing the things you could get into when you knew the man inside out. If his father was one thing, it was predictable. The combination hadn't been difficult to figure out, with his mother's help. He sighed heavily. *His mother*.

When he'd arrived back at the mansion in White Plains, the only demand he'd made was that his father return her medication. On opening the door to her room, he'd found her curled in the fetal position on the bed, shaking violently and muttering incoherently. It was those four days during which he held her in his arms as the drugs seeped back into her system, that he swore to himself he was never going to allow his father to hurt her, or anyone else, ever again.

This past week he had returned to the office, where the jungle drums had remained far from quiet and who he was had become common knowledge. He'd sat the men down and explained everything to them. Far from being shunned as he'd rightfully expected to be for his subterfuge, they'd offered him only support and comfort. Although they had been unable to give him any information on Vance and Audrey as they had been bundled into another SUV soon after Adam had left with his father. All Graham had said was that Vance looked about as devastated a man as any he'd ever seen.

It was with Graham's help and his contacts around the building, that Adam had finally found the information he'd been searching for, which had ultimately led him to the paperwork now in his possession. Well… copies of the paperwork. He wasn't an idiot. He'd covered his tracks, even though his father had been watching him like a hawk. He only hoped it would be enough to convince Vance he was telling the truth.

The plane landed with a bump and the usual screech of tires as the pilot applied the brakes. Adam looked out of the window at the tarmac rolling by as they taxied to the terminal and tapped his fingers impatiently on the arm rest while he waited for the seatbelt sign to be switched off. His journey was almost over. He'd already rented a truck and once he was behind the wheel, he would be only two hours away from Wolf Creek, and Vance. Providing the cowboy didn't make good on his threat and shoot him.

Adam eased the SUV to a stop and switched off the engine. He stared at the house for a few moments, gathering his resolve. This was not going to be easy. But then he was expecting nothing less. He'd hurt Vance. In the worst way, and he was going to have to work damn hard to convince him he was sorry. But if he didn't try, he'd spend the rest of his life regretting not taking the chance.

As he opened the door and stepped out onto the ground, his backpack in hand, light flooded the entrance and the main door flew open, slamming on its hinges. There he was. Big, beautiful, and mad as hell. Adam took a deep breath, walked toward the porch and climbed the steps.

Vance stared him down, his expression warring between painful betrayal and explosive anger. Adam wasn't entirely sure which one scared him the most—although it was probably the barrel of Vance's shotgun currently trained on him that was winning. Swallowing against the lump in his throat, Adam squared his shoulders and stood his ground. He wasn't going to let Vance chase him away—not this time. The silence between them stretched to breaking point and when it became obvious Vance wasn't going to be the one to speak first, Adam moistened his lips.

"We need to talk."

"We're done talkin', *Mr Blackwell*." Vance's response was delivered with a sneer, his lip curling in anger. "Now get off my land."

"No." Adam said firmly and, before he knew what he was doing, he'd slapped the end of the gun, almost knocking it from Vance's hands. "And don't point that fuckin' thing at me unless you intend to use it."

"What the fuck is wrong with you?" Vance stared at him open-mouthed. "You *never* make a grab for the end of a gun! What if it had been loaded?"

"It's not loaded?"

All Vance's anger seemed to dissipate, quickly replaced with irritation. Which Adam took as a good sign. If he was irritated, he still cared. "Of course, it's not fuckin' loaded. Don't flatter yourself," Vance snapped. "I haven't shot anyone yet, and I sure as hell ain't startin' with you."

"For which my bladder and I are eternally grateful."

"The fact that you thought it might be, no matter how briefly, just proves how little you really know me."

Adam nodded toward the front door. The debate on how well he knew Vance Wolf was one he really didn't have time to enter into right now. "Can I come in? We need to talk. Audrey, too. She's going to want to hear what I've got to say."

"There's nothing you have to say that either of us wanna hear."

Barging past Vance, Adam stepped over the

threshold and into the big square foyer. "Trust me, you're going to want to hear this."

"*Trust* you?" Vance strode into the house and slammed the door behind him. "That's a mighty interestin' choice of words, coming from you."

"For God's sake!" Adam's frustration boiled over and he grabbed two handfuls of Vance's shirt, getting right up in the cowboy's face. "If you *couldn't* trust me, would I be here now? Would I ever want to set foot on this stupid property again? When is your goddamn stubborn pride going to let you see what's really going on around you? I've come here at not only great personal risk to myself, but also to my mother, to make sure you don't get swindled out of what is rightfully yours!"

Vance's tone could have frozen the warmest heart, icicles hanging on every word as he said menacingly, "Take your hands off me."

Dropping his hands, Adam took a deep breath then turned on his heel and headed down the corridor to the kitchen. Audrey looked up from the kitchen table where she was reading a magazine, a cup of coffee in her hand mid-way to her lips as he walked in. Her gaze widened and the cup clattered back into its saucer. He knew he'd find her in here. It was the heart of the house, just as she was the heart of the family.

"Adam. What are you doing here? Does Vance know?" Audrey made as it to rise to her feet and Adam quickly shooed her back down into her chair.

"Don't get up," Adam said softly. "I just want to talk." She sank back into her seat and he took the one opposite her. "And yes, taking into account the shotgun he pointed at me, I'd say he knows." He knew by the way her gaze shifted to something over her shoulder that Vance had crept into the kitchen with his usual cat-like stealth.

"Shotgun?" Audrey was horrified. "Vance Elvis Benjamin Wolf, you pointed a shotgun at him?"

"Don't get your panties in a bunch, Momma," Vance said petulantly. "It wasn't loaded."

"I don't care," Audrey replied. "It's the intent that concerns me. I thought I raised you better."

"Hold on, now." Adam tried to control the twitching of his lips as Vance stared at his mother in amazement. "He's the one that lied—to *both* of us—and *I'm* the one gettin' my ass chewed?"

"You know how I feel about guns."

"This is totally fu—fudged up."

"Shut up," Audrey said to her son, her tone brooking no argument. "Adam came all the way out here to talk, so the least we can do is listen—then you can kick his lying ass out if you want—but there'll be no shooting in my house."

It was Adam's turn to stare at the seemingly frail woman sitting at the head of the table. Oh, how misleading a gingham apron and a soft smile could be. He sighed heavily. "I guess I deserve that." Shifting uncomfortably under their icy stares, he amended, "Okay, I *definitely* deserve that. But not everything was a lie." His gaze sought Vance's. "*I* wasn't. I didn't lie about us."

"I ain't got time for self-serving sermons," Vance drawled sarcastically. "Just say what you came to say and get out."

Adam's gut tightened. It wasn't as if he was surprised at Vance's behavior. Hadn't he expected him to react this way? Of course, he had. But he hadn't expected every hate filled look to rip into his heart and leave a jagged tear. He took the papers out of his jacket pocket and put them on the table in front of him.

"I want you both to know that I had no idea when I first got here that my father owned the Garton place. I only learned that from the ledger I found in Vance's office, but once I'd found out, I couldn't understand why. Why would he buy a ranch? He's a businessman, not a farmer, and—more to the point—why did he want *this* one? Your beef is good, but the Andrew Blackwell I know would be far more interested in eating it than raising it. Which got me to thinking there had to be something else. Something more important than the cows. Important enough for him to use not only my anonymity at work and my sexuality, but my mother against me to force me to dig for the answers he wanted. So, I started digging—literally. I just dug for a lot more than whether you were making ends meet.

"After I left here, I spent the first week with my mother, getting her medication back in her, waiting for her to come back to me. Then I returned to the office and began rooting around. Anyway, to cut a long story short, I finally found what I was looking for in the safe in his office."

"You broke into his safe?" Audrey reached out and curled her fingers around his. "Adam, what if you'd been seen? He could have hurt you."

Adam shrugged. "I was hurting already. It didn't matter." He stared at Vance, who dropped his gaze to the tabletop, and his gut tightened. "In the safe I found a file full of papers and reports on the Garton place. At first, I couldn't believe what I was seeing, it seemed so impossible. But after I'd made a few phone calls and found out how willing people are to give information to a Blackwell; I knew it was true." He scrubbed a hand over his face, his gaze once again zeroing in on Vance. "Since you weren't taking or returning my calls, I got on a plane and came straight here to tell you what I'd found."

Audrey stood up and Adam watched her cross the room to the fridge. She opened it and removed a large glass jug filled with homemade lemonade. She took a glass down from one of the overhead cupboards and filled it before putting the jug back into the fridge and returning to her seat. She pushed the glass across the table to Adam and then said, "Tell us what?"

"The reason why my father wanted the Garton's and this place so badly." Adam drank hungrily. The ride in the car had been dusty and he'd not had any fluid since he drained that bottle of water on the plane. The lemonade slid over his tongue and down his throat, lighting up his taste buds and making them sing.

"Which is?" Vance asked impatiently.

Adam leaned forward and fished the file out of his backpack. Opening it, he pulled out the report and pushed it across the table to Vance, where it slid into his coffee cup.

"Adam?" Audrey's voice jolted him from his reverie.

"There's only one reason my father bought the Garton ranch and wants Wolf Creek so badly."

"Again, I say," Vance growled. "*Which is?*"

"Gold."

Chapter nine

"Gold." Vance stared at Adam, his jaw hanging open on its hinges. What the fuck was this guy smoking? "Gold?" He knew he was repeating himself, but the concept was so ridiculous he couldn't stop. "*Gold?*"

"Doesn't matter how many times you say it, cowboy. It's still gonna be true."

"You're a complete whack-job." Vance shook his head in wonder, his gaze flitting from Adam to his mother and back again.

"Maybe not."

Vance stared at his mother; whose expression was thoughtful instead of the completely aghast it should be. "What do you mean, 'maybe not'?" he snapped. "Don't tell me you're actually buying this crap?"

"Well…" Audrey stood up and crossed the kitchen to the percolator and poured three fresh cups of coffee. When she was once again seated at the head of the table and they each had a steaming cup in front of them, she began to tell a story… a very old story.

"Aloysius Garton laid claim to the land adjoining ours after Benjamin Wolf had already picked this parcel for himself. In one of his diaries, Benjamin stated that he only thought it fitting since Aloysius was his best friend, and living next to each other, raising their children together, was something both men looked forward to. Unfortunately, it didn't quite turn out that way.

"Aloysius and Benjamin had a falling out over who the creek actually belonged to. Technically it was on Aloysius' land, but the creek's origin was in a rock formation to the east, on Benjamin's property. It came down those rocks and disappeared below ground. Then it appeared back above ground further along the valley and flowed downstream to form the creek." Audrey paused and took a mouthful of her coffee.

The fine hairs on the nape of Vance's neck began to take an interest in the proceedings and stood up to pay attention. Goose bumps broke out all over his bare forearms. Was she saying what he thought she was saying?

"Anyway, the fight continued for the rest of their lifetime, and they never spoke to one another again. But nowhere in any of Benjamin's diaries did it say why they fought over the ownership of the creek, or what it was about the creek that was more important to them than their friendship." Audrey shrugged. "I mean, there *were* stories floating around over the decades. Some said we were sitting on top of a copper mine, some said there must have been oil, or gas, and some even mentioned gold."

Vance stared at his mother, the silence in the room growing heavy, thickening the air around them. He huffed out a laugh. "Bull-crap." His gaze settled on Adam. "Bull-*crap*. Don't you think if anything was out there it would have been found already?"

"I'm just telling you what I know," Audrey said, curling her fingers around her coffee cup. "All I'm saying is, knowing what I know the possibility isn't that far-fetched… is it?"

"Then why hasn't anybody found it before?" Vance ran his fingers through his hair, agitated.

"Maybe, like you," Adam said, leaning forward in his chair. "They all thought it was bull-crap. Probably brushed it off as an old story that got mixed up with Chinese whispers over the years and it was forgotten. I don't have *those* answers. But what I do have is the jar you're holding, and the chemical analysis report. Whether you choose to believe it or not, cowboy. There *is* gold in them thar hills."

Vance's head was spinning like an out of control top. *Gold? Seriously?* Blackwell wanted to buy the land because he thought there was gold on it? His father was driven to an early grave for stupid chunks of metal? Vance's blood began to boil in his veins, white hot. His fingers curled into fists where they lay on the tabletop. When he found his voice, it didn't sound like him, not even to his own ears. "My father *died* because the great Andrew Blackwell wanted more *money*?"

"Vance."

He ignored his mother and slammed his fist down onto the table, making the cups rattle where they rested. "Answer me!"

Adam ran a hand through his hair and Vance watched as he seemed to sink inside himself. Adam's voice was so low, he had to strain to hear it. "Yes." When they looked into his, Adam's eyes were filled with pain. "And I could never tell you how sorry I am for everything you've lost through his actions—*never*."

Vance had to get out. The room was closing in on him. He felt stifled—couldn't breathe. He stood up so fast the chair clattered to the floor behind him. The sound rang loud in the quiet of the room. He shook his head, wanting to say something… *anything*. But he couldn't think of any words to describe the emotions battling inside him. He turned on his heel and strode from the kitchen, ignoring his mother's pleas and the sound of Adam calling his name. He'd opened his heart to this man, and he'd lied to him, over and over. Adam had come here to make sure they weren't swindled out of everything they were entitled to? What they were entitled to? Did Adam think that *really* mattered?

The sounds and smells of the barn assaulted his senses as he strode through the doors, letting them slam behind him. Vance's feet carried him to Goliath's stall, and he grabbed the bridle hanging on the hook by the stall door. His need to be surrounded by the open plains, the wind on his face, overrode the instinct to saddle Goliath completely. He quickly slid the bit between the horse's teeth and the straps of leather over the beast's head. Leading Goliath out of his stall, Vance gasped at the huge clap of thunder overhead. Which was almost drowned out by the heavy slamming of the barn door. He glared at Adam, noting the anger on his face and in his steps as he stomped toward him. Vance turned away and stepped up onto a box to mount Goliath's broad back. The shove came as a surprise and he lost his balance, fell off the box and landed on his back in a pile of hay.

"What the fuck is wrong with you!" Vance yelled, scrambling to his feet.

"You are *not* running out on me again!" Adam could yell just as loud. "*Talk* to me." The way his voice broke on the last word was like a punch to the gut for

Vance, but he couldn't deal with Adam's pain right now. There was only his own.

"I can't."

Vance grabbed the bridle again and attempted to mount Goliath for the second time. Once again, he found himself on his ass in the hay. "Adam," he warned as he got to his feet. *"Don't."*

"Why?" Adam stepped into Vance's personal space and glared at him. "You gonna hit me?"

"Adam."

"'Cause that's the only way you're getting out of this barn, cowboy." Adam ended his threat with a poke to the chest and Vance tried to keep control. "Talk to me. Scream at me. Do whatever you need to do, I don't care. You're hurt, I know that, and I'm sorry. I wanted to tell you. But I couldn't. He had my mother locked in her room going cold turkey without her meds. What the fuck was I supposed to do?"

"Adam… please." Vance couldn't hear this. Didn't want to hear this.

"Do you think you're the only one who lost here?"

Vance stared at him open-mouthed. "You're kidding me, right?" he spluttered. "My father *died* because of your father's *greed*. What the fuck did you lose? Top billing in the will?"

"*You*, you fuckin' asshole!" Adam practically screamed at him. "I lost *you*, and whatever this was, or could be." His hand shook as he waved it between them. "Everything we had a chance of becoming crumbled the moment I saw my father's name in your dad's ledger. Why do you think I ran for my life, for God's sake? But you just kept coming."

Vance shook his head in disbelief. "What are you

saying? That this is my fault?" He stabbed an agitated finger at Adam's chest. "*You* wanted us as much as I did."

"I'm not saying that!"

Adam scrubbed his hands through his hair, and an unbidden memory of the light strands against the contrasting color of his suntanned skin bounced around Vance's skull, a memory he quickly shook away. If he stopped being angry long enough to listen to the racing of his heart and what *it* wanted— Vance swallowed hard. How could he even think like that? His father was in the ground, and Adam was a part of the man responsible. How he *felt* didn't matter—not anymore.

"I'm saying it's my fault." Adam's voice held a note of desperation. "I'm saying I thought if I was with you, just once, I could walk away without a backward glance. That we could both walk away intact. But in here, that night, watching your heart break over losing Midnight, I saw the real you and I knew right then that walking away was not an option for me. I was going to tell you the truth about everything. About who I was. About what I'd done, hoping I could do something, anything to make you understand, and then my father showed up."

"Stop… *please*." Vance forced the words past the lump in his throat, hating the raw, broken sound they made on the air. The rain had begun while Adam was ranting, and it clattered onto the roof like someone throwing stones. "I can't deal with this. Not now." His breath hitched in his throat. "I can't look at you without seeing *him*. Don't you see? Don't you understand what I've *done*?" All he'd wanted to do was run, now the words flowed from him as though a faucet had been turned on, and he couldn't reach it to shut it off. He scrubbed his hands over his face, anguish filling his very soul. "I knew who I was before I met you. Then you came with that smile and that goddamn attitude and shook everything up. I've never wanted a relationship before. I go out, I hook-up, I come home. No strings, no emotions. But with you," he swallowed, "it was different, right from the start, and I wanted all of it. All of *you*.

"Then I found out who you were, and nothing made sense. What kind of man was I, that I could have put my own wants ahead of my loyalty to my Dad? He was my best friend my whole life. Taught me right from wrong, how to tie my shoelaces, how to rope my first calf, and how did I repay him? Instead of gettin' him the justice he deserved, what did I do? Fell for the son of the man who put him in his grave." Tears spilled over his lashes and down his face, but he ignored them. He was past caring. The guilt he felt over wanting Adam… needing Adam, had been eating him up. Hollowed him out and left him an empty shell. "How could I want you?" he sobbed. "How can I *still* want you? Why does every bone in my body *ache* for you, even after everything your father has done to my family?" Vance felt all the fight go out of him and he slumped backward onto his ass in the hay behind him. He stared desolately into space, not really focusing on anything around him. "I thought I was a stand-up guy, but now… I don't even know who I am."

"Well, I do." Adam sank to his knees beside him in the hay, and cupped Vance's face in his hands, forcing him to look at him. "You're Vance frickin' Wolf, the orneriest cowboy in the whole damn state. You're beautiful, inside and out, with a capacity for love that takes my fuckin' breathe away every time I see you. And you're the man I *really* tried not to fall in love with. But I couldn't have stopped it anymore than I could have stopped the world from turning."

"But—"

"Vance," Adam's voice was soft, but firm. "We're not our fathers, and I'm no more responsible for my father's actions than you are for yours. I can't bring your dad back. I wish I could. *God*, more than anything I wish I could, and if I spent the rest of my life saying sorry it still wouldn't be enough. But I can love you, if you'll let me. And we can build a life together. A life of our own. A life that's ours. A life that's not tainted by the Blackwell name." He shrugged and Vance saw the anger leave him, too, and he stared at the sudden terrified vulnerability on Adam's face. "That is… if you want to."

Could they get past it? Vance gazed deep into Adam's eyes and the love he saw there broke through the wall he had built around his heart. Adam was right. There was only one man responsible for Blackwell's actions, and that was Blackwell himself. He'd find a way to make him pay, but right now was their time— his and Adam's. With a half-sob and a half-sigh, Vance cupped Adam's face and pulled him in, and kissed him.

Chapter ten

Adam stood in front of the mirror and studied his reflection. He looked the epitome of everything his father disapproved of most. The T-shirt he wore was faded by years of wear, his jeans the same, the knees frayed and revealing his skin beneath. Not exactly the corporate suit his father was used to seeing him wearing. His hair had grown out a little since he'd first arrived at Wolf Creek and he couldn't arrange it in its usual crisp, neat style. Bangs flopped onto his forehead and the sides were beginning to curl around his ears—something his father hated with a passion. The haircut makes the man was a view held very close to whatever it was that Andrew Blackwell had where a heart should be. His cowboy boots were scuffed and dusty, and his wrists were adorned with the thin leather bracelets his fellow learner cowboys had given him on Friday when he'd said goodbye to his old life.

Today was a big day. For the first time in his life, he was standing up to his father. Was he scared? Damn straight he was. Was he going to go through with his plan? Fuck *yes*. He sighed heavily, wishing he didn't look as terrified as he felt. The last three weeks had been spent flying between the office in New York during the week and the ranch at the weekends. He'd needed his father to believe everything was as normal as possible while he'd made all the necessary arrangements. Adam checked his watch. Arrangements that should already be underway. The ball had started rolling and it was gathering speed, with only one more piece of the plan to slot into place—his father. Who would be arriving at Wolf Creek any minute now.

"Are you sure you're ready for this?"

Adam had been so lost in his own thoughts he hadn't heard Vance come back into the room. He smiled at Vance's reflection behind his in the mirror. Vance's arms slid around his waist and Adam leaned into the cowboy's embrace, letting him take his weight for a moment. He was more than grateful for the relief, unsure if the wet noodles that used to be his legs would hold him up for much longer. "What did Marla say about Donatello?"

Vance's gaze in the mirror was locked firmly on his. "Nice try," Vance said, raising a sardonic eyebrow, "but I ain't biting."

"Yes." Adam turned in Vance's arms and slid his fingers into Vance's hair. "I'm *sure*." He pulled Vance's head down and nipped playfully at his chin, soothing his tongue over the hurt he caused.

"You're tryin' to distract me, aren't you?" It wasn't a question.

Adam smiled against Vance's skin. "Is it working?" He gasped as Vance grabbed his hand and rubbed his palm over the bulge in Vance's jeans.

"What do you think?"

"I think you should start countin' cattle, cowboy, 'cause we don't have time for any funny business." Adam tried to pull his hand away and groaned low in his throat when Vance held him fast, grinding his hips into Adam's hand. "You're a bastard, you know that right?"

Vance guided him to the bed and eased him back onto the mattress. "Yep."

Adam sighed into Vance's kiss, opening up to the nudge of his tongue. Every time Vance kissed him it felt like the first time. He had no idea how Vance managed to pull it off. But if he was honest, he didn't really care—as long as Vance just kept doing it. He hooked his leg over Vance's hip and arched into the thigh that pressed between his, hands buried in Vance's hair, tilting his cowboy's head so he could hold him to get the best angle on his mouth. *God.* How he loved this man. Although they'd only known each other for a relatively short amount of time, Adam could barely remember what his life was like before Vance was in it. His hands fell from Vance's hair and onto his shoulders when Vance broke the kiss and turned his attention to the throbbing pulse in Adam's neck. When he thought of how close he'd come to losing him… He swallowed hard, blinked at the sudden prickling behind his eyes and turned his head.

"Hey," Vance said, pushing himself onto his elbows and forcing Adam to look at him. "What is it?"

Adam shrugged and huffed out a laugh. "I'm just being stupid." He brushed Vance's bangs from his forehead and frowned. "I love you. You know that, right? No matter what he says, or what he does, I need to know that you won't let him make you doubt that."

"Are you kidding me?" Vance sat up and yanked Adam into sitting beside him. "You've given up everything. For *me*. There is nothing *anyone* can say, or do, that could ever make me doubt how you feel."

Adam's heart swelled. Vance preferred to express the way he felt physically. To hear him vocalize his feelings meant more than Adam could ever explain. But he knew his father better than Vance did. After he heard what Adam had to say, Andrew Blackwell was going to come back all guns blazing. Adam could only hope he had the strength to stand his ground.

"You can do this."

"Get out of my head." Adam smiled and traced the outline of Vance's lips with his forefinger. "Freaks me out how well you know me."

"Well enough to know how your father makes you feel." Vance kissed him with such a tenderness that Adam had trouble swallowing past the sudden lump in his throat. "But like you said before, you're not him. You could never be him. There's more integrity in your little finger than there is in that man's entire body. You're a good man, Adam Prentiss, and you've got one thing that your father definitely doesn't have."

"What?"

Vance grinned widely and Adam couldn't help but return it when he said firmly, "Me."

"That's true," Adam said. "And what an asset you are."

"Hell yeah," Vance countered, pushing Adam back onto the bed. "I have many extremely *useful* assets."

Adam hooked his leg around Vance's waist and neatly rolled him over. Something he could only do when Vance was least expecting it. "And what are those again?" What the hell, they probably didn't have time, but the tease was too delicious to resist. He dipped his head and captured Vance's full lower lip between both of his own, swiping his tongue along the tender flesh. "Your mouth?" He whispered the question and then deepened the kiss, swallowing Vance's moan as he plundered said asset. He drew back slowly when he'd had his fill—for now—Vance's lip between his teeth, stretching the flesh a little before he let it go. "Mmm, yeah, definite asset. But not my favorite…."

He trailed off, dragging his blunt fingernails down Vance's torso until he reached the wolf's head buckle on Vance's faded leather belt. Adam licked his lips as he drew the shape of Vance's shaft pressing against the button of his fly. "Now this… *this*… is one hell of an asset." He slid his palm along the bulge and heat surged through him as Vance thrust into his hand, green eyes darkened, lips parted, breath hitching in his throat. Knowing he could reduce the cowboy to a quivering mass of need with a few words and touches, made him feel as though he could conquer the world.

"Adam… *please*." Vance's voice cracked on the please, the word filled with need.

Adam didn't need any other invitation. He all but ripped Vance's jeans open and pulled the waistband of his boxers over his dick and tucked it behind Vance's heavy balls. For what he had in mind, it was all the naked he needed.

He leaned down and pressed his lips to Vance's, his voice husky and low as he whispered, "When he's spewing his vitriol, I want your taste on my tongue, your scent on my breath, your seed coating my throat. I want to know that every time you look at me you can feel my mouth on you, sucking you down, making you mine, making me yours."

"*Yes*." Vance's affirmative was almost feral in its intensity and his dick twitched in Adam's hand. "God,

Adam, *fuck yes*! Take it. Suck me."

Adam scrabbled down the bed and took Vance between his lips in one smooth move. The heavy weight of heated flesh on his tongue made his own cock scream for attention. The scent of musk and sweat made his senses sing. So good, so fucking good, with Vance's name a mantra in time with his racing heart.

Adam bobbed up and down on Vance's shaft, taking him in as far as he could, curling his fingers around the rest. He cupped Vance's balls in the other hand and set up an overload of stimulation with as much rhythm as he could maintain, sucking, kneading and twisting until Vance begged him for release. But he didn't let him have it. He took him to the edge and back time and again, until Vance had begun to let out a litany of curse words that would make a sailor blush. He squeezed the base of Vance's shaft and lapped at the thick vein running the length of Vance's dick, and stabbed his tongue into the slit at the crown. And all the while he kept Vance's orgasm at bay with the pressure of his fingers.

"Adam, baby… please… I gotta… you gotta… *please*, baby… fuck… *please*."

Adam smiled against Vance's flesh, his pleas like music to his ears. He sealed his lips over the head of Vance's dick, loosened his grip, hollowed out his cheeks and sucked—hard. It was all over. Vance pumped hot strings of cum into Adam's mouth, losing control as he thrust mindlessly. Adam groaned as the bittersweet taste of Vance's essence slid over his tongue and down his throat. He swallowed every drop, not wanting to miss one single second of the delicious tang that was unmistakable cowboy.

When Vance had finished, Adam kitten-licked at his softening dick until Vance batted at his head in complaint, mumbling something about being too sensitive and death by orgasm. Adam chuckled softly and let Vance's dick from fall between his lips with an obscenely wet sound. He was as hard as nails in his jeans, but that wasn't important. Not as important as the pleasure that still twitched in Vance's muscles as he lay, utterly spent, staring unfocused at the ceiling. He gently pulled Vance's boxers back over his dick, then buttoned his fly and buckled his belt, before sliding back up Vance's body to kiss him soundly. "You okay?"

Vance sighed contentedly. "You are *way* too good at that."

"I try to ma—"

Wheels churning up the dirt outside the window as a four wheel drive passed the window sounded loud in the stillness of the room. Adam didn't finish his sentence. The words effectively cut off by the sound, the post-orgasmic glow very much interrupted.

"Daddy's home."

Adam stared down at Vance, noted the smirk on his face and couldn't help the snort of laughter that bubbled up his throat. "Come on, cowboy." He stood up and straightened his clothes, ran his hands through his hair.

Vance stood up and laid his palm to Adam's cheek, smoothing his thumb across Adam's lips. "You ready?"

Adam squared his shoulders and nodded. "Let's finish this."

He heard his father's voice as they approached the kitchen and couldn't stop the flashback to the last time

Andrew Blackwell had been in this house. His entire world had come crumbling down around his ears when he'd walked into the kitchen that day to find his father sitting at the table, his lips curled in that all too familiar smirk. The unbidden memory faltered his step and Vance bumped into him. Vance grabbed his arm to steady him when Adam stumbled.

"I've got you," Vance whispered. "Always."

Adam nodded and took a couple of deep cleansing breaths. Then he offered up a silent prayer to the God of whatever that his now jelly-like legs would hold him up long enough to do what he needed to do. The voices became louder as they neared the open doorway and Adam could hear the sarcasm that laced his father's words.

"It's nice to see your son has finally come to his senses, Mz Wolf. You won't get a better offer for this… *concern*."

Adam stepped into the room, followed closely by Vance. "Hello, Dad."

Andrew Blackwell's head turned so quickly; Adam was surprised he didn't get whiplash. His father's eyes widened. The smug expression gave way to one of such utter confusion and bewilderment, it was almost laughable. Bizarrely, it was that faintly comical moment that seemed to lift some of the weight of Adam's shoulders. For the first time he saw his father for what he was. A bully, the wrong side of fifty, who used his money and standing to get what he wanted. But all that was about to change. The warmth of Vance's hand on the small of his back seeped into his skin. He wasn't alone anymore, and his father couldn't hurt him, or those he loved, ever again.

"Adam?" Blackwell frowned, his gaze flitting between Adam and Vance. "You're in New York."

"Not today."

Blackwell's gaze narrowed, and the speed with which his face became its usual emotionless mask was impressive. Adam had to give him that. But then if his father was anything, he was first and foremost a consummate businessman. A role he was well versed in playing.

Adam sat down at the table opposite his father. He noted the way his father's gaze followed Vance as he sat down beside Adam, undoubtedly taking in the hand on Adam's back, the way Vance moved his chair closer to Adam's, and how Vance made sure their shoulders touched when he was seated. He recognized the tension in his father's jaw and knew, despite the cool, calm exterior, his father was furious. He wasn't used to being played—and he definitely didn't like it.

"Nice outfit," Blackwell drawled. "Should I have brought my chaps and chewing tobacco?"

Vance mock shuddered. "You in chaps? I think I just lost my appetite—forever."

"Funny." Blackwell crossed his arms and leant back in his chair. "Now we've got the niceties out of the way, perhaps you'd be good enough to tell me what I'm doing here?" He raised a sardonic eyebrow. "We'll get to what *you're* doing here later."

"Well I can answer that last one straight away," Adam said, trying not to flinch beneath his father's withering stare.

"Is that right?"

"I live here."

Blackwell's eyes darkened menacingly, the only

outward indication of his anger. "I beg your pardon?"

Adam swallowed, grateful for Vance's hand on the back of his neck. "I live here. With Vance. He's my partner. My lover. We have sex." *Oh my God. Stop talking you ass!*

"I think he's got it, babe," Vance said softly.

"Thank you, Mr Wolf. Adam obviously doesn't have much faith in my powers of deduction." Blackwell's tone was as cold as ice. "Mz Wolf, could I trouble you for some of that fabulous lemonade you're so famous for? I'm not used to the dust and my throat is a little dry."

Adam glanced at Audrey, who looked as though she'd rather tip lemonade over Blackwell's head, rather than in a glass. But of course, she wouldn't. Her southern manners, ingrained by her mother and her grandmother before that, wouldn't allow her to.

"Of course, Mr Blackwell." Audrey's reply was said so sweetly, sugar dripped from every word as she stood and crossed the kitchen. The three men stared at each other in silence while they waited for her to return to the table with a tray laden with a huge jug of lemonade and four glasses.

Adam's stomach churned nauseatingly. He could do this. He knew he could. But that didn't mean there wasn't a real possibility he might throw up while doing it. He picked up the lemonade Audrey put in front of him and downed half of the glass in two large gulps. The glass clattered slightly when he put it on the table, due to the tremor in his fingers and cursed inwardly. A glance at his father's face told Adam he'd heard it and was amused by what he no doubt saw as weakness.

Blackwell sipped at his lemonade and cast his most

charming smile at Audrey. "You really should think about bottling this stuff. You'd make a fortune." He turned his attention back to Adam. "I don't know what you're playing at, boy. But I think it's time you explained yourself. I repeat, what am I doing here?"

"You are here to discuss an offer, that much is true. But not your offer—mine." It was all Adam could do to hold his father's gaze. The disapproving weight of that stare was crippling.

"*You* have an offer for *me*?" Blackwell laughed heartily. "What on earth could you possibly have that I'd want?"

"Your reputation."

Blackwell leaned forward, his gaze narrowing. "I'd advise you to be very careful, son. I'd hate there to be any unforeseen consequences to your actions."

"There's nothing you can do to me that you haven't done a million times over." Adam didn't even try to keep the sneer from his voice.

Blackwell chuckled again. "I wasn't talking about *you*."

Adam's gut tightened. The threat in his father's voice loud and clear. He didn't need anything spelled out for him. He knew exactly who he meant. Adam's mother. But now, for the first time in his life—it was his turn to laugh. "I know you weren't. But that's one piece of leverage you no longer have."

"What are you talking about?" There was the barest flicker of confusion in his father's eyes, and it gave Adam renewed strength.

Adam glanced at his watch. "At eight-thirty this morning, half an hour after you left for the airport, a moving company arrived at the house and began loading all of Mom's things into their truck. Right about now, she should be enjoying a relaxing cup of her favorite herbal tea in her brand new home."

"You're lying."

"Call her if you don't believe me."

Adam watched as his father calmly reached into his pocket and pulled out his cell phone. He stabbed agitatedly at the numbers and put the phone to his ear, waiting for the call to connect. Adam's stomach lurched uncomfortably at the change in his father's expression, when the automated voice told him the number he'd called was no longer in service. As Adam had known it would.

"Oh, that's right. I forgot. New number." Adam's stomach lurched but he kept his composure. One crack and his father would be on him like a lion on a distracted gazelle and leave his throat open and bloody for all to see.

"You pathetic little queer. Do you really think you can best me? She'll be back where she belongs by tonight."

"I don't think so, Dad. Not this time." Adam leaned back in his chair and laid his hand, palm up on the tabletop, smiling softly when Vance immediately accepted his open invitation and curled long, tanned fingers around Adam's. "You see, I may have more Blackwell in me than either of us thought. When you sent me here on your little digging trip, I did some of my own. You can imagine my surprise when I found out you owned the Garton property. I mean, what the hell would *you* want with a cattle ranch? Let's face it, Dad, you're more Boston Legal than Bonanza." He took another chug of lemonade before continuing.

"Anyway, like I said, I did some digging and found a few invoices to a geologist in New York. Invoices for soil and core rock analysis on samples found in the creek. The secretary at the firm you hired was more than happy to help explain exactly what those invoices were for when she realized I was simply following up some accounts at my father's request. You know, it really is amazing what effect the Blackwell name has on people. I really should have taken advantage of it more often. I could have gotten some really nice tables at swanky restaurants."

"Adam—"

"He's not finished." Vance cut off Blackwell sharply, then smiled at Adam. "Go on, baby."

"Why, thank you, honey," Adam drawled in his best imitation of a Texan accent, and was rewarded by the darkening of Vance's gaze—although his was definitely not in anger. "As I was saying. She was more than helpful and said the invoices were for samples analyzed to determine whether or not there is gold in the creek. Talk about a wild card! I'm telling you, Dad, of all the reasons I could possibly imagine why you wanted not only the Garton property for, but this one as well, I gotta say, *gold* wasn't even on the list."

"Adam." Another clear warning.

"Hey, I'm impressed, seriously. But then I got to thinking, okay, there's gold in the creek, which runs right next to the Garton property. That's obviously why you bought the ranch. But why would you want Wolf Creek if the gold was on the Garton side? Then it came to me. Maybe the source of the gold *wasn't* on the Garton side after all. Maybe, just maybe, it came from rocks washed down into the creek from Wolf land. If it was, that would make sense why you wanted Wolf creek so badly. So badly that you were willing to do *anything*, including stealing, poisoning and haranguing a good man into his *grave*, to get what you wanted. Am I getting warm, Dad? Or should I go on?" Adam's voice had risen on every point, until he was almost shouting the words by the time he'd finished. But his father's face remained an impassive mask. "For God's sake, Dad. Say *something*. Show some kind of *emotion*. Anything to indicate that you actually give a shit about what you've done—to this land, to this *family*, to *me*!"

Blackwell picked up his drink, the silence deafening as he drank his fill, then put the glass back down. He took the folded handkerchief from his top pocket and patted his lips then leaned back in his chair. "That was a very heartfelt and emotional speech, Adam. Now I have something I'd like to say."

Adam swallowed. "Which is?"

"Prove it."

"I can't," Adam replied. "Not in a court of law anyway." He paused. His father wasn't the only one good at ramping up the tension. "But in the public arena... I'm sure I could throw enough dirt to make some of it stick for a very, very long time."

"What are you saying?"

"I'm saying, if you don't accept the terms of my offer, I'll go to the press."

"You don't have the balls," Blackwell sneered.

"Try me," Adam said firmly. "I'll ruin you. You'll be a laughingstock. The company's existing clients will jump ship. New clients will go elsewhere, not wanting their name associated with yours. The rumor mill will be rife, you'll be black-listed at the country club.

Imagine it, Dad. Do you really think people are going to want to line the pockets of a thief propelled by greed… a murderer… a wife-beater… a homophobic child abuser? You're precious fuckin' standing in the community won't count for shit. Hell, by the time I'm finished, the Blackwell name won't even get you a table in McDonalds."

"You wouldn't dare." Blackwell's famous mask was beginning to crack. "You're not strong enough to go the distance, boy. You're like your mother. Weak and pathetic. Spineless. Do you think I can't squash you like the insect you are? I'll tell them how this, this… inbred, ingrate," he waved a hand at Vance, "turned you against me, forced you to say unspeakable things about your own father. I'll be pitied and revered, supported by everyone who knows me when they see how I had to all but kidnap you and put you into a secret treatment facility. They'll see what a loving father I am as I nurse my darling boy back to health, my faithful wife by my side, while the beast who brainwashed him languishes in jail." He glared at Vance. "Pick your crime, Mr Wolf, I can make all of them stick." Blackwell's gaze flitted back to Adam. "You can't beat me, son—and you know it."

Adam reached out and curled his fingers over the rim of the ceramic bowl Audrey kept filled with fruit in the middle of the table and pulled it toward him. "I know, Dad," he said, nodding his head in agreement. "Which is why I needed a little insurance." He watched with satisfaction as his father's face visibly paled when Adam pulled out the tiny recording device he'd hidden amongst the fruit earlier. A press of the button to rewind the tape and then another to play and Blackwell slumped in his chair, the sound of his own voice echoing in the silence of the kitchen, *"While the beast who brainwashed him languishes in jail. Pick your crime, Mr Wolf, I can make all of them stick."* Blackwell knew it was over, Adam could see it all over his face and for the first time in his life, his father looked old. For the briefest of moments, he felt a twinge of pity for the relationship they could have had, *should* have had, but it was too late for that now. He brushed the thought away.

"What do you want?" The defeat was there in Blackwell's voice.

Vance's fingers tightened on Adam's and he returned the pressure. It wasn't quite finished. "Firstly, you will not attempt to find Mom—ever. You will sign any paperwork received by your lawyer, including financial settlement requests, and give her the chance at the life she should have had, not the nightmare you forced her into. Secondly, the members of my team will remain in the firm's employ for as long as they so desire, with their salary to be increased by ten per cent for the duration." He swallowed past the lump in his throat. It was nearly done. "Thirdly, you will sell the Garton place with all its mineral rights to Vance Benjamin Elvis Wolf for the sum of one dollar. I've had the paperwork drawn up. All you have to do is sign it. Once you've done that, you will get in your car and off this land. And if you even entertain the idea of setting foot on it again," he smiled at Vance beside him then stared directly into his father's eyes, "I *will* let him shoot you.

"If you do not accept the terms of the offer as I have laid them out for you; I'll take this tape to every newspaper who'll print it—so everyone will know what kind of man you really are." Adam took the document Audrey handed him and pushed it across the tabletop to his father. Then he sat back and waited.

He didn't have to wait long.

Blackwell took a pen from his inside pocket and picked up the printed pages. He didn't even look at Adam, simply signed the document where it was marked and then shoved it back across the table.

Adam checked the papers were signed correctly and nodded in satisfaction. He folded them in half and then handed them to Vance before turning his attention back to his father. Blackwell stood up and straightened his jacket, brushed an imaginary blemish from the lapel, his eyes cold and dead—a shark's eyes.

"Too bad it took you so long to grow a pair, Adam," Blackwell said, his tone scathing as his gaze wandered over Adam one more time. "I would have been proud for you to carry the Blackwell name. A name and the prestige that goes along with it, of which you will no longer receive the benefit."

"I don't want it," Adam said vehemently. "Goodbye, *Mr.* Blackwell."

Blackwell turned on his heel and strode from the room. Moments later they heard the heavy front door slam behind him.

Vance's arms came around him with such force he nearly knocked Adam off the chair. "You did it! You were fuckin' awesome!"

"Vance!"

"I'm sorry, Momma, but he *was* fuckin' awesome!"

Audrey smiled softly and nodded. "Yeah, he was fuckin' awesome, alright."

Adam buried his head in Vance's shoulder and held on for dear life. His entire body shook as he crashed from the adrenalin that had been surging through him. And, bizarrely, he could feel tears pricking behind his eyes. What the hell was he crying for? He'd done it. He was the victor. His father was out of their lives forever. His mom was safe, and he and Vance could start to build a future together. Who was making that noise? It sounded like a wounded animal. Where the fuck was it coming from? It wasn't until Vance murmured over and over, close to his ear, "I've got you, baby," that he realized the wounded animal was him. Sinking into Vance's warm embrace, Adam cried. For everything he'd lost, for everything he'd never had, and for everything his father had done. Cried until there was nothing left.

Adam leaned against the corral fence. Raphael and Mike were frolicking together, kicking up a dust cloud while Goliath and Jupiter looked on with disdain at the young-uns. He chuckled as Raphael tried to coax Jupiter into the game and the old man responded with a snap that missed Raphael by inches, but he heeded the warning nonetheless and rejoined Mike at the other end of the corral.

The years of heartache and despair he'd released after his father left had been cathartic, cleansing, and he felt lighter than he had in a very long time. Vance had held him until the tears had subsided and he'd been heaving dry, hiccupping sobs like a small child. He'd tried to struggle free from Vance's arms a couple of times, embarrassed by his own weakness, and not entirely sure why he was crying in the first place. But his beautiful cowboy had refused to let him go, murmuring soothing nonsense and holding him fast. At that moment, Adam couldn't have loved him more if he'd tried.

Adam gazed at the horizon over the miles of fields stretching beyond the ranch. Watching the sunset had become a habit since he'd come back to Wolf Creek. The way the big orange ball of fire dropped slowly behind the hills and cast pink and red across the valley took his breath away every single time. Tonight's sunset was no different. It amazed him how much he had come to love this beautiful place, and how he couldn't imagine himself anywhere else.

He started when strong arms wrapped themselves around his waist and Vance dropped his chin onto his shoulder. Adam sighed contentedly and rubbed his cheek against Vance's, reveling at the feel of the cowboy's rough stubble against his skin. "I love it here," he murmured softly into the night air.

"I'm kinda fond of it myself," Vance chuckled, pressing a kiss to Adam's ear.

"So, what happens next?"

"What do you mean?" Vance asked.

"Well, I may have been cut off," Adam said with a shrug. "But that doesn't mean I don't have enough money to get professionals in to look for that gold. The samples were analyzed, and it *is* out there. We just have to find it." After a long pause, Vance replied.

"I've got everything I want right here." Vance's arms tightened around Adam's waist and he nuzzled at his jaw. "That gold has caused enough trouble over the last hundred years. I reckon it's better off where it is."

"I love you." Adam turned in Vance's arms and slid

his arms up around his neck.

"I love you, too," Vance said softly, and pulled Adam tight against him. "And I never thought I'd be saying that to no *city-boy*. I musta been damn loco when I roped you."

"Roped *me*?" Adam said, mock affronted. "I think you'll find it was I who roped *you*."

"Is that so?" Vance said with a sly grin. He removed Adam's arms from around his neck and walked across to the barn.

Adam frowned in confusion, wondering what the hell the lunatic was doing now. But when Vance returned with a lasso in his hand, he laughed, long and hard. "You're crazy."

"*I'm* crazy?" Vance said, tossing him the lasso. "You roped me, huh? C'mon, City-boy," he crossed his arms, "show me exactly how you did that."

Shaking his head, Adam lifted the rope and stared at it, letting his fingers slide along its length. There was no instant tightening of his chest, no difficulty in breathing, no heaviness around his wrists. He wasn't afraid anymore. A smile curving his lips, he began and began to spin the loop above his head, faster and faster, picking up speed—then threw it. He'd closed his eyes at the crucial moment, of course, but when he opened them the rope was around Vance's shoulders. "I did it!" he crowed, bouncing excitedly. "Did you see that? I actually did it!"

"Pure luck," Vance complained. "You had your eyes closed, for Christ's sake!"

"Luck, huh?" Adam yanked on the rope. The lasso tightened on Vance and he was forced to take a step forward. A wicked smile curved Adam's lips as he reeled Vance in, pulling on the rope until they were so close barely a breath could come between them. He leaned up and captured Vance's lips in a kiss that left them breathless and shaking. "You sure about that?"

Vance shrugged off the rope and pressed his thigh between Adam's, swallowing the moan Adam couldn't contain as he rubbed against Vance's leg, desperately trying to get friction where he needed it most. Adam almost sobbed when Vance pulled back, but his smile mirrored Vance's when he said softly, "You know what, City-boy? We might just make a cowboy of you yet."

THE END

Also by Lisa Worrall

Available from **White Stiletto Press:**

Always Hope
Is Love Still Enough?
Summer Heat
Not Just for Christmas
'Tis the Season
Too Much Christmas Spirit
A Nanny for Nate
Westford Hall
In the Heat of the Night
Halfway House
New York Cowboy
Behind the Mask
U.S. Male
Ed & Fred are... Dead
Follow My Lead
What's the Worst that Could Happen?
Forever Dusk
Marshall's Park
Solo Honeymoon
Running from the Past
Mr. Popsalos – Book One and Two
Unshakeable Faith
Thirst (Re-release coming soon)
I Can See for Miles (Re-release coming soon)
Before Sundown (Re-release coming soon)

Laurel Heights Series:
Laurel Heights Book One
Laurel Heights Book Two
Laurel Heights Book Three

**Left at the Crossroads Series
by Lisa Worrall & Sue Brown:**
Book 1 - Un-Expected by Lisa Worrall
Book 2 – In-Decision by Sue Brown
Book 3 – Un-Deniable by Lisa Worrall

Available from **Triskell Edizioni**
Una Tata Per Nate
Hope
Laurel Heights
Laurel Heights 2
Laurel Heights 3 (Coming Soon)

Available from **Juno Publishing**
Enquête à Laurel Heights
Enquête à Laurel Heights 2
Enquête à Laurel Heights 3 (Coming Soon)
Crépuscule éternel

Available from **JMS Books LLC**:
"Frozen Angel" in Tea and Crumpet

Available from **UK Mat Publishing**:
"Reunion" in British Flash (Free Read)

Available in print:
Always Hope

Summer Heat
Westford Hall
A Nanny for Nate
New York Cowboy

Marshall's Park - The Complete Series
Laurel Heights
Laurel Heights 2
Laurel Heights 3
Unshakeable Faith
Solo Honeymoon
Thirst
The Gardener and The Movie Star

Awards:
Unshakeable Faith
Rainbow Awards 2012
Honourable Mention
and One Perfect Score

Laurel Heights 2
Rainbow Awards 2015
Honourable Mention

About Lisa Worrall

My home is in Leigh on Sea, a small seaside town just outside London on the coast of Essex, about ten minutes from Southend, which boasts the longest pier in the world. I live with my husband and two teenagers who refuse to stop growing, who I let think are the boss of me; along with a mad-as-a-box-of-frogs fat dog, who actually is.

I adore horror movies and thrillers with more twists and turns than a helter-skelter. I also have a penchant for tattoos and singing at the top of my voice in the car – to the constant embarrassment of my children – and my guilty pleasure is the Antiques Roadshow and the occasional custard cream.

My passion, however, is making sure two gorgeous guys get their happy ever after. Come along for the ride. Drop me a line at:

Website: http://lworrall.blogspot.com
Facebook:
https://www.facebook.com/lisa.worrallauthor
Facebook group:
https://www.facebook.com/groups/2951763673260
40/?ref=bookmarks
Twitter: https://twitter.com/Lisa_Worrall
 Email: lisaworrall69@gmail.com